Romance Unbound Publishing
Presents

The Auction

Claire Thompson

Edited by
Donna Fisk
Jae Ashley

Cover Art by Kelly Shorten

ISBN 978-1480112148
Copyright 2012 Claire Thompson
All rights reserved

Chapter 1

"The last man who bought me kept me chained by the wrists to a bar inside a closet when he wasn't using me. I would fall asleep on my feet, surrounded by his clothing." Jessica, one of Carly's fellow slaves-in-training at the auction house, closed her eyes and sighed dramatically. "He was *so* hot, though. The time spent in the closet was *well* worth the wait, let me tell you." Jessica leaned back in the huge hot tub, sliding down until only her head showed. The tips of her white-blond hair darkened to honey as they floated on the frothing water.

Cassandra, a redhead with breasts as round and hard as cantaloupes interjected, "Hey, at least he was good looking. The guy I had last time was at least twice my age. He must have weighed over three-hundred pounds. Even his ears were fat! The only thing tiny on that guy was his dick."

All five women soaking in the tub laughed at this, but beneath the laughter Carly sensed the others shared her edgy excitement. Even the women like Cassandra and Jessica who had already been successfully auctioned in the past were still required to undergo the week-long slave training, though for them it was just a refresher, while for Carly the experience had been intense and rigorous. She had managed to get into the program under somewhat false pretenses, and as she listened to the women share their prior experiences, she wondered for the hundredth time that week if she was getting in over her head.

"Let's go, girls. Free time is over." Mistress Audrey entered the large communal bathroom where the young women had been given their first half hour of free time since they'd arrived for training seven days before. All conversation instantly ceased, as the slave girls were not permitted to speak in the presence of their trainers, except in answer to a direct question.

Mistress Audrey was dressed in her usual black Spandex tank top, a riding crop tucked into the waistband of her leggings. Despite her outfit, Mistress Audrey always reminded Carly of a queen, the tilt of her chin and the toss of her head regal and utterly commanding. At the same time, she was gracious and patient, which Carly especially appreciated, being one of the new kids on the block.

The next hour passed in a whirlwind of hair styling, makeup and last minute instructions by both Mistress Audrey and Master Franklin on auction decorum and expectations. At the stroke of eight, Master Franklin announced, "It's time. Remember all you've learned. I trust you will prove yourselves worthy. Hopefully each one of you will have a new Master tonight." If Mistress Audrey reminded Carly of a queen, Master Franklin would have been one of her knights, a guard with his sword ever at the ready, his feelings kept well in check behind a stern expression that betrayed no hint of emotion.

The slave girls were led onto the small stage, each girl taking her place on the silk cushion placed on the side stage, back straight, head bowed. As Master Franklin greeted the gentlemen sitting at tables in front of the stage, Carly tried to remember how to breathe. Butterflies were batting wildly in the cage of her stomach. She experienced a sudden, nervous urge to giggle.

Despite the relatively modest exterior of the building that housed *Erotica Auctions*, the auction room had been decorated like something out of a nineteenth century mansion, with real crystal chandeliers, Persian carpets over polished wood floors and deep wingback leather chairs. Original oil paintings of nudes reclining on silk settees or the soft moss of riverbanks hung in gilded frames on the walls, and there was a marble fireplace with a huge mirror above the mantle set in an elaborately ornate antique silver frame. The room smelled of leather, lemon oil and the lingering smoke of fine cigars.

Though she knew better, Carly dared to turn her head slightly, giving her a view of the auction room and the ten men who made up the night's select clientele, one of whom, she both hoped and feared, would take her home that evening.

Her eyes lingered on a man in the center of the room. He had thick black hair that curled against his neck, clear gray eyes and a strong chin. He was dressed in the understated elegance of the truly wealthy—cashmere, finely spun cotton and loafers Carly guessed cost a month's rent. He held a brandy snifter in one hand, the other resting lightly on the leather folder Carly knew contained all the pertinent details about the five women who were up for bid, including explicit photos in leather and rope, detailed descriptions of each woman's health record and experience level in BDSM, and what she was seeking in a potential Master.

As she stared at the man, he turned as if aware of her gaze and looked directly at her. Carly knew she should look away, should look down at the ground as she had been instructed to show her submission and respect, but she couldn't seem to tear her eyes from his face. He continued to stare at her, giving her the oddest feeling that he was looking past her face and into her secrets.

Master Franklin touched Carly's shoulder and squeezed. She felt the warning in his fingers and, face blazing, quickly averted her gaze, focusing on the royal blue cushion beneath her knees.

The first potential slave put up for bid was Angie, a voluptuous beauty. She was naked, as all the girls were, and boasted long black hair that cascaded down her back in shiny waves. Her skin was dark and smooth, her features exotic, with almond-shaped eyes and sensual, pouting lips. She moved gracefully, without a trace of self-consciousness as she was ordered to pose in various positions that intimately revealed her many attributes.

As she moved with languorous ease, arching her back, spreading her legs, turning to show her ass to the men and bending forward to grasp her ankles, the auctioneer directed the bidding and the men called out their offers. After several minutes, the auctioneer hit his gavel against the podium, the sharp crack of wood on wood making Carly jump.

"Slave Angie is awarded to Mr. Chapin for thirty-four thousand dollars." Master Franklin approached Angie, clipped a leash to her collar, and led her off the stage.

Oh my god, I'm next.

"Our second lovely slave girl of the evening is slave Carly," the auctioneer announced, punctuating his words with another sharp tap of the gavel. Carly looked at Mistress Audrey, who nodded. Her heart knocking against her ribs, Carly rose unsteadily from her kneeling position, praying no one could see that her legs were shaking. She followed the trainer, trying to walk in the swaying, lilting way she had been taught by the trainers.

Carly came to a stop at center stage and turned to face her audience. Though they'd been kept naked or nearly so for most of the week, Carly felt more exposed at this moment than she ever had in her life. While she had grown increasingly comfortable with her constant nudity, now that she was standing naked and alone on the stage, it was all she could do to resist covering her body with her arms and turning away from the hungry gazes of the men staring up at her.

Yet when Mistress Audrey tapped her shoulder with the end of her riding crop, the week's constant training kicked in and Carly sank obediently into a kneeling position on the stage floor, keeping her back straight and eyes downcast.

Another tap and Carly spread her knees to give the men a better view of her shaved pussy. She held herself still, her chin raised. She focused on the middle distance, carefully avoiding eye contact with the man with the dark hair who sat only a few feet away, brandy and cigar in hand. When she felt two taps on her shoulder she rose with as much grace as she could muster on legs that felt like rubber.

A tap to her upper arm, and Carly placed her hands behind her head, lacing her fingers together as she displayed her naked body for her potential Masters. A tap on her back and she turned, hands still behind her head, thrusting her ass out toward the men as she'd been taught. Finally she bent as Angie had, grasping her ankles, glad the men couldn't see her face, which from the scalding heat on her cheeks she knew was beet red.

Another tap, and Carly turned slowly back toward the audience while Mistress Audrey addressed the men. "You have Carly's detailed information in your folders, but as quick recap, she is thirty-two years old, five foot six and weighs one hundred twenty-two pounds. This is Carly's first time with *Erotica Auctions*, but if she pleases you, we are hopeful this won't be her last."

Was Mistress Audrey really talking about her? Was Carly really up there on the stage waiting to be handed off to the highest bidder? How surreal this felt, displaying herself like a slave girl in Ancient Greece. "She is available for the standard one-month contract," Mistress Audrey continued, "with renewal terms to be negotiated."

Though Carly kept her eyes down, she felt Mistress Audrey move away and her heart, which was already pounding, leaped into her throat as the auctioneer said, "The bidding begins at twenty thousand."

"Twenty-one," called out a voice from a far corner of the room.

"Twenty-two," called out another. Carly had the odd sensation that she was standing outside of her body, watching this bizarre event unfold as if it were happening to someone else. She wanted to look up, to see who was bidding, to see if the man with the gray eyes was one of the three voices that kept calling out their bids, but she didn't dare.

"Thirty," came the voice from the corner. In the silence that followed Carly bit her lip so hard she nearly broke the skin. The auctioneer hit the gavel. "Going once…"

"Fifty thousand dollars," said a new voice, its timbre deep and pleasing.

There was sudden hush in the room as if everyone, Carly included, were holding their breath. Carly's heart beat against her sternum as she stood in front of the men, feeling as if her very life hung in the balance as the auctioneer waited for another bid.

Finally she heard the strike of the gavel. "Slave Carly is awarded to Mr. Wise for fifty thousand dollars."

As Mistress Audrey approached her, Carly couldn't help it. She looked up, her heart lurching as she saw the handsome man with the gray eyes getting to his feet and moving toward the stage.

~*~

Adam Wise wasn't quite sure what had compelled him to jump in with that winning bid. The slave girl he'd just purchased wasn't even his physical type. He favored slim, small-breasted women like slave Nina, a twenty-four-year-old beauty who seemed to have a submissive streak a mile wide. He had focused on Nina's dossier and had planned to bid on her and only her.

Yet when the five women had been led out, for some reason he was drawn to the woman kneeling to Nina's left. He recognized her from the photos as Carly, with her unruly tumble of curly, golden brown hair and vivid blue eyes set in a heart-shaped face. She looked younger than her stated age of thirty-two, and where Nina exuded exotic sophistication, Carly looked more like the fresh faced girl next door, too puppy-dog eager for Adam's tastes.

Yet he'd been captivated when she turned her head, sneaking a glance at the men who were ready to shell out a sizable sum to take a woman home for a month as their submissive sex toy. Not that fifty thousand was all that much in the scheme of things, not when you were worth millions.

There was something in her gaze that caught and held his attention, a kind of secret fire behind those innocent blue eyes that he wanted to explore further. After all, it wasn't as if he were choosing a life partner, or even someone to drape on his arm at the endless events he was obliged to attend in his role as business magnate. This girl was just a toy—an amusing diversion he would use for a month and then forget. Not one to lose out on what he wanted,

Adam made his bid high enough to shut out the others around him.

Now he sat across from the woman, whose nakedness was covered by a white satin slip that clung alluringly to her curves. She kept biting her lower lip, and her hands were playing nervously with the silver pen resting on the table in front of her.

Franklin Jasper also sat at the table. He was a tall, lean man with iron gray hair and a stern visage, his lips drawn down in a perpetual frown, deep lines bracketing his mouth. He put his hand on the papers in front of him.

"This is the final draft of the contract, compiled based on our discussions, Mr. Wise, and on Carly's prior agreement to the basic terms."

He pushed a copy toward each of them. "Please read it over. You've both already agreed to the basic protocol, conditions, duties and responsibilities. This just ties together the loose ends. Mr. Wise, you have the original, slave Carly, you have a copy. Mr. Wise, once you approve of the content, please sign where indicated and pass it over to the slave for her signature."

Adam picked up the contract and began perusing it, glancing as he did so at Carly, who was staring down at her copy. Her curls had fallen over her face so that he couldn't see her eyes. Her mouth was slightly pursed as she concentrated, the tip of her pink tongue appearing between red lips.

He looked again at the pages in front of him. He was already familiar with much of the content, as it had been developed and discussed with him during the week leading up to the auction, but he skipped to the page he hadn't seen, which included Carly's hard limits. He was pleased to see she had only one: *don't break the skin or draw blood*. This made sense to Adam, and he approved.

He picked up the pen that had been placed beside the contract, his hand hovering over the signature line as the enormity of what he was committing to sank in fully. The whole bidding idea had begun as a kind of lark when he'd first heard about the BDSM auction. "Why not?" he'd joked at the time. "Women are only after my money anyway. We might as well be upfront about it."

But now, sitting across from the woman who was, for all intents and purposes, entrusting her life to him for the next thirty days, it didn't seem like a joke at all. He was going to have total control over her, and be completely responsible for her, a woman he knew next to nothing about, except that she was a submissive masochist and willing to sell her charms for a hefty fee.

Well, this was what he'd wanted, wasn't it? A submissive sex slave to play with to his heart's content, and then send packing before she tried to weasel her way into his heart, or far more likely, his wallet.

Forget the romance, the wooing and the waiting games. He'd gone down that road one time too many in his forty-one years. No, this was much cleaner and more honest on both sides. A transaction between informed and willing parties. What could be simpler?

Taking the pen, he signed the document and slid it toward the girl.

She met his eyes for a moment, and behind the nerves he could see gritty determination and a certain strength. Seeing him regard her, she looked quickly down, reaching for the pen. Her hand shook very slightly as she signed. What was going through her head, Adam wondered. Was she as aware as he was of the import of what they were doing?

Franklin, who had risen from his seat, was suddenly beside Carly. He took the contract and put a hand on Carly's shoulder. "You now belong to Mr. Wise. You are his property. Kneel on the carpet at once and keep your head bowed."

Carly slid from her chair and knelt with her back straight, her curls again obscuring her face as she looked at the ground. Franklin continued to address the girl, "You no longer have any say over your person or your actions for the next month, except as Mr. Wise permits. While this is not, strictly speaking, an enforceable contract in a court of law, it is binding insofar as any breach of the terms of the contract during its time frame will result in forfeiture of all monies owed, and you will not be permitted to enter another auction with us *ever*. Your portion of the award money will be kept by *Erotica Auctions* for you until the successful completion of your slave term. Is that clearly understood?"

"Yes, Master Franklin," the woman said to the floor. Based on her nervous mannerisms, Adam had expected her to squeak, but her voice was sultry and sexy in a way that went directly to his cock.

Turning to Adam, Franklin said, "I'll make a copy of this contract for our records, and get Carly's suitcase. I won't be a moment."

Left alone, Adam regarded the kneeling girl. Her head still down, he saw that she was again worrying her lower lip and he thought of kissing that luscious mouth then and there, but controlled himself. The contract had said nothing of kissing. Whipping, binding, fucking every possible orifice, yes, but kissing—was that considered too intimate? The irony of that at once amused and irritated Adam, and to distract himself from this line of thought he barked, "Stop that."

The girl looked up. "I'm sorry, Sir, stop what?"

"Stop biting your bottom lip. It's very unattractive. I can't believe your trainers didn't beat that out of you on day one."

"Oh!" Carly touched her mouth with her hand. "Please forgive me, Master."

"Hands at your sides." Adam snorted. "And don't call me that. I'm Adam. Or Sir if you absolutely insist. You are Carly. Is that understood?"

"Yes, Mas—Sir."

She looked down again. Her cheeks were flushed, her nipples visible beneath the silk slip. Adam sat in silence watching her. What in the world was going through her head? Beneath her submissive façade, did she regard him with contempt, even hatred?

What did it matter? This wasn't a love match, nor was it permanent. *Erotica Auctions* had represented these slave girls as of the highest caliber in every respect. If he was unhappy, he'd been assured, he could sever the contract and get his money back, less the quite substantial nonrefundable deposit, naturally. Still, with that kind of cash changing hands, he doubted they would be offering up inferior merchandise.

She was guaranteed disease-free and she was on birth control. Not only that, she'd signed the waiver regarding condoms, which pleased Adam, as he abhorred the annoying little things. Who cared if her submission was genuine or just an act? He would get his money's worth—he would see to that.

Adam's thoughts were interrupted as Franklin stepped back into the room. Adam stood as he entered, accepting the contract the trainer handed him and folding it into the inner pocket of his jacket. Franklin handed him Carly's suitcase, which Adam took, wondering what was inside. Whatever was in there, she wouldn't be needing much. He planned to keep her naked, save for leather, rope and chain.

Franklin extended his hand. "It's been a pleasure doing business with you, and I trust you'll find full satisfaction with slave Carly."

Adam shook the man's hand. "Thank you. I intend to."

Once Franklin had gone, Adam turned to Carly, still kneeling quietly on the carpet. "Take off that collar. You'll wear this instead." Adam reached into his pocket and held out the collar he'd chosen for his slave girl.

Carly reached behind herself, her hands slipping beneath her thick hair to unbuckle the slim strip of black leather from around her neck. She let it fall to the ground and, lifting her hair from her neck, she bent her head forward in a submissive gesture that pleased Adam.

Bending down, he buckled the soft red leather collar around her throat and placed a small padlock through the clasp at the back of her neck, clicking it into place. Using the O ring at the front of the collar, he pulled Carly to a standing position. The red collar looked pretty against her white throat.

She was barefoot and clearly naked beneath the thin slip. It was a warm September evening and the car was parked just outside the building, so Adam supposed that was all right. "My driver's waiting outside," he said. "Come, Carly. It's time to see your new home."

Chapter 2

Carly stole sidelong glances at Adam Wise as his driver sped along the Bronx River Parkway toward the Scarsdale residence where she would be spending the next month. She liked the way his hair curled against the side of his neck. He had a good jaw and a prominent, slightly crooked nose. She guessed him to be in his late thirties or early forties, and he was in good shape. Yeah, he was probably just another rich, entitled bastard, but at least he was hot. She was glad he'd bought her, instead of the fat redhead with the freckles.

Bought her...

I can't believe I'm really doing this. I am out of my mind. Crazy as a loon.

Melissa, the bartender at *Club de Sade* where Carly had managed to get a job as a waitress, had told her about the slave auctions and said they were always looking for beautiful, submissive women to train. At first Carly had just laughed, dismissing the idea out of hand.

When Melissa had mentioned the sums involved, and what a girl could earn for one month of "work", Carly had stopped laughing.

"Is that even legal, though?" she questioned. "It sounds like prostitution, plain and simple. How can they get away with that?"

Melissa shook her head. "It's a service, that's all. Think of it like a dating service, except with a kink," she'd grinned. "They just bring people together, really. What those people do in private is no one's business. It's a lot safer than just meeting some random guy at a BDSM club, when you think about it. The clients are as carefully vetted as the girls. They have to provide proof that they're disease free and undergo a thorough background check for any criminal record. And they're all loaded—they have to be with the prices the auction house charges."

Carly had been laid off eighteen months prior, when the law firm she had worked for had closed its doors, and the unemployment had run out four months ago. She was already two months past due on her share of the rent for the house in Queens she shared with three other women. They had been understanding at first, but were now telling her to come up with the money or get out. She couldn't blame them, but even working the part-time retail job she'd recently managed to garner plus the weekend waitress gig at the club, she could barely keep her head above water. Spending a month as some rich guy's submissive sex slave and standing to earn more from that than she had in the past year suddenly didn't sound so terrible.

Carly glanced again at Adam, disconcerted to realize he was staring directly at her. She looked quickly down at her lap.

Adam hadn't said a word since they'd gotten into the car, and following his lead, neither had Carly. Now he put his hand on her leg, pushing the satin of her slip upward as he stroked her thigh. Her initial impulse was to push his hand away — she barely knew the man — but of course she did no such thing. She was property, his property, bought and paid for. She wasn't about to fuck things up right out of the gate. If he wanted to touch his property, he had every right.

Think of the money, she reminded herself. *Thirty-five thousand dollars will go a long way to getting you back on your feet.*

Adam took his hand from her thigh. "Face me," he ordered.

Though she was in her seat belt, she managed to turn herself toward him. His eyes glittered in the glow of the streetlights zooming past. He reached for her breasts with both hands, finding and twisting her nipples beneath the silk until she gasped in pain. She shot a glance at the driver, wondering if he could see them in his rearview mirror.

"Keep your eyes on me," Adam said, twisting harder. Carly winced and sucked in her breath.

Despite the pain, or partially because of it, she felt her cunt moistening. While he tweaked and twisted her nipples, Adam stared into her eyes, and again, as she had at the auction, she got the disconcerting feeling that he was staring past them into her mind, into her darkest secrets.

He let her go, leaving her nipples throbbing and engorged. "Sit back and face front."

Carly's heart was pattering rapidly as she shifted back against the leather. Unbuckling his seat belt, Adam slid closer to her, re-buckling himself in the middle seat so their legs were touching. Again Adam began to stroke her thigh. She looked down at his hand. It was rugged and masculine, the skin tan against her pale skin. His nails were well tended and he wore no rings.

His hand moved higher, his fingers stroking the inside of her thigh. Carly bit her lip and then remembered his earlier admonishment to stop doing that. His touch was light and sensual, and in spite of her nervousness, she had to admit it felt good.

"Spread your legs," he said in a low voice.

Carly did as she was told, her heart kicking into a higher gear. Adam's fingers edged toward her cunt, grazing the outer labia.

"Lift your slip. Ass on the leather and keep your legs spread." Carly felt heat licking her cheeks and throat and silently admonished herself to get over it.

The week of intensive training at the hands of Master Franklin and Mistress Audrey had knocked a lot of Carly's natural modesty right out of her. She and the other women who'd stayed in the dormitory at the rear of the auction building, or the slave quarters as they were grandly referred to, had been kept naked most of the time, even during meals.

Yet somehow it had been different there, with all the other slave girls around her. It was the natural way of things in that environment. It had been more like a game, albeit a very intense one. But here in this elegant sedan beside this rich, handsome stranger, with another strange man just a few feet away, felt nothing like a game.

Carly lifted the hem of the slip, settling her bare bottom against the soft, luxurious leather.

"Wider." Adam punctuated the command with a light slap to her inner thigh.

Carly looked down at Adam's hand as it moved over her shaven sex. He cupped her there, his palm pressing against her clit. He pushed one finger gently inside her and Carly felt the involuntary clamp of her vaginal muscles. Keeping his finger inside her, he moved his palm in a circular motion against her spread labia.

Carly sighed with pleasure, shifting slightly against his hand.

"Don't move," Adam said softly. "Don't move a muscle. No matter what I do."

Carly nodded, catching her lip with her teeth, remembering and letting it go again. She closed her eyes.

"Keep your eyes open. Look at me. I want to see your face."

Carly turned her head toward Adam, another soft, moaning sigh pulled involuntarily from her as he slid a second finger carefully inside her and ground his palm against her clit. The combined sensation sent shivers along her nerve endings. She felt the raw power emanating from Adam, sparking like dark fire in his eyes, and she found herself drawn to him in a way she hadn't expected.

Her body wanted to move—her hips wanted to lift and swivel against his hand as he stroked her from within and without, but she forced herself to stay still. "Oh," she gasped, her voice tremulous with the effort of keeping her body still.

The slave girls had rarely been permitted to orgasm during their week-long tenure, though they'd been sexually tortured and teased to teach them restraint and discipline. Several of the women were able to orgasm on command, or at least fake it really well, but Carly had never mastered either skill. She didn't come easily to orgasm and she could never bring herself to fake it, no matter how much she wanted to please a man.

There would be no need to fake tonight, that was for sure, not with what he was doing to her. A rushing, steady heat was building inside her at his touch, and the way his eyes seemed to drink her in only added to the pulse of intense sensations. His touch was light, but steady and persistent, his palm pressed with precisely the right force against her swelling sex while his fingers moved like a cock inside her.

Don't stop, don't stop, don't stop.

Carly realized her mouth was open, her breath coming fast and shallow. She forced herself to slow her breathing, trying to draw more air into lungs that felt constricted by the pounding of her heart. She could smell the scent of her own sex in the air of the enclosed car. She could hear the squishing sound his fingers made in her now sopping cunt as he moved relentlessly inside her.

She blinked rapidly in her effort to keep her eyes open and fixed on this enigmatic stranger who was pulling so much from her with just his hand. She was powerless to stop the panting and little mewling sounds she heard herself making. Adam's eyes continued to burn into hers, his mouth lifting into a small, knowing smile.

After several minutes of this silent, exquisite torture, Carly's body began to tremble and a low, feral moan escaped her lips. Still he continued, stroking her both inside and out.

"Oh!" The word burst from her as her disobedient hips rose to meet his hand. Despite the constraint of the seatbelt, Carly was thrashing like a wild animal in heat as a powerful orgasm tore its way through her helpless body. It was as if he was striking her with a kind of lightning, the currents moving from his hand to her body, burning her to her core. She realized her eyes were squeezed shut, tears running down her cheeks, as wave after wave of white-hot pleasure hurtled through her loins.

When he finally released her, Carly sagged back against the seat, her breath rasping in her throat, her chest heaving, her body still shaking. All the training and discipline of the past week had completely deserted her in the face of Adam's skilled, relentless attentions. She had, she knew, fucked up big time, and right out of the gate.

Shit. Shit, shit, shit, shit.

Struggling to sit upright, she turned a beseeching gaze to him. "I know you said not to move. I tried, I really did. I couldn't help it. I'm sorry, Sir."

One corner of Adam's mouth lifted in an ironic, cruel smile. "Not nearly as sorry as you're going to be."

~*~

Adam watched Carly's eyes widen as she stared around the front hall of his home, her mouth actually hanging open in evident awe. *Pygmalion meets Pretty Woman*, he thought with an inward grin.

Jordan had parked the Mercedes and gone up to his apartment over the garage, so they were all alone in the big old brownstone, just Adam and his purchased slave girl.

It was after eleven but Adam didn't feel in the least tired. He made his own schedule, and he'd cleared the next week completely. Sleep could come later. Right now he had other plans.

Setting Carly's suitcase on the floor, Adam said, "I would have thought a trained sex slave would have more discipline than you showed in the car." In fact he was delighted with how responsive she'd been to his touch. One of his fears in making this unorthodox purchase was that he'd get someone who could take pain and perform sexually, but who would only be going through the motions. What had just happened in the car was something else again. Not even the most skilled actress could simulate the orgasmic flush that had seeped over Carly's skin, or the way her pupils had dilated so wide, or the trembling that had racked her body in small, seismic waves. As he'd played her to his tune, he'd felt that delicious rush of pure power moving through him like a drug.

"Yes, Sir, I'm very sorry, Sir," the girl began in a rush of words. "I didn't mean to. It won't—"

Adam held up a palm. "Stop. Not another word."

Carly pressed her lips together, and Adam had a sudden vision of her on her knees, his cock rammed down that pretty throat. Why not make it a reality?

"Take off that slip and get on your knees. I'm going to outline the rules."

He reached for his belt and quickly unbuckled it, pulling at the zipper of his fly and tugging his underwear aside. His cock sprang out, his erection as hard as an eighteen-year-old boy's.

Carly pulled the flimsy garment over her head and dropped it to the floor. She'd been naked on the stage, but close up she was even more breathtaking. Though he didn't usually favor such buxom curves, on this girl they worked, and how. Her breasts reminded him of lush, round melons, and his mouth actually watered at the thought of taking those dark pink nipples between his teeth. Her waist was tapered, her hips flaring into a feminine curve. Her shaved cunt pouted prettily between her thighs.

She knelt in front of him on the marble, staring with wide eyes at Adam's cock. "You know what to do," he said.

Pink color washed over Carly's cheeks. Adam was both amused and surprised at this blushing maiden business from someone who'd just sold her body and her rights to a stranger for cold, hard cash.

Leaning forward, Carly closed her mouth over the head of his cock. She started to reach for him with her hands but Adam stopped her. "Only your mouth," he ordered. "Show me some of that skill the trainers promised me."

He sighed with pleasure as she moved her head downward, her hot little tongue stroking the underside of his cock as her lips massaged him. He reached for her hair, gripping handfuls as he pulled her head toward him, forcing her to take the length of his shaft deep into her throat. He was pleased when she didn't gag. Her throat muscles were relaxed as she accepted him and her mouth felt like hot, wet silk as she suckled him.

As much to forestall his orgasm as to educate her, Adam began to outline the rules he'd been thinking over in the car. "Keep focused on what you're doing," he told the girl whose head was bobbing at his groin, "but pay attention to what I'm saying. For the next month you will observe some basic rules of the house." He paused a moment, savoring the hot, sweet mouth surrounding him.

"You will not sit on any furniture without express permission or direction. You will ask permission to eat, drink, sleep, use the toilet, shower, speak and orgasm. I may or may not grant that permission, and you will abide by my decision."

He groaned softly as she did something especially skillful with her throat muscles. At this rate he was going to come too quickly. He pulled back, trying to focus on what he was saying. "I have a cleaning crew come in a few times a week, but you will be responsible for making the bed and keeping the bathroom spotless. You will also keep your body smooth and clean at all times."

She was licking just the head of his cock, her tongue sending shivers down the length of his shaft. Adam tried not to pant as he continued. "You will sleep at the foot of my bed. I expect to be awakened by your mouth on my cock. My seed will be the first thing you taste each morning. I will mark you with a single tail and then you will shower. You will present yourself for inspection afterward. If you pass inspection, we'll have breakfast and then I'll take you to the dungeons for your morning torture session."

The image of this lovely girl strung up in his dungeon, her naked body crisscrossed with welts, her cries heard by no one but him, made his balls go tight. He grabbed Carly's head and pulled her down onto his shaft, using her hair to hold her in place while he thrust in and out of her soft mouth.

This time he did gag her, but he didn't care. This felt good, so good, and he wanted to come, he needed to come so he could concentrate. His cock was thrumming, his balls tight. All at once he pulled out, letting his jism land on her face and breasts and the floor between them.

She remained still, her lips shiny with saliva, her hair a tousle of unruly curls around her face, her chest heaving. Adam tucked himself back into his trousers. When he could catch his breath, he pointed to the blobs of ejaculate on her breasts and cheeks. "Swallow it. Every bit of it."

She hesitated, a flash of distaste moving over her face, but then she began to obey, swiping the goo from her body with her left index finger and placing it into her mouth. Adam made a mental note of the hesitation, for which she would be punished.

Meanwhile he said, "The floor too. Lick it up."

Again the slight hesitation, but she knelt forward, shoulders to the cold marble, her pretty pink tongue lapping at the few drops that had splattered there. When she was done, she sat back on her haunches. Adam knew her knees had to be hurting from the hard floor, but to her credit she said nothing.

He crouched on the floor in front of her. Lifting his hand, he slapped her face hard. She jerked her head to the side and gasped, her hand flying to her face. "Hands at your sides," he barked, and he slapped her again, just as hard, on the other cheek.

Tears sprang to Carly's eyes, but she kept her hands down. Her cheeks were bright red and a single tear slipped down her face. Despite his recent climax, Adam's cock nudged at the pretty sight.

"That was for hesitating," he explained. "When I tell you to do something, you do it. Understand? My word is law. Break that law, and pay the price."

He stood and reached his hand down to her, indicating she should take it. He pulled her to her feet. "Speaking of breaking the law, that was a very undisciplined display in the car. Tell me, what were my instructions?"

Carly looked down, mumbling something.

He reached for her chin, forcing her face up. "Speak clearly."

"I moved, Sir. You told me to stay still, no matter what you did to me."

"That's right. And what happens to slave girls who don't do as they're told?"

Her voiced trailed to a whisper. "They get punished."

Adam's smile was wicked, his cock tingling at the prospect. "It's time you saw the dungeon."

Chapter 3

Adam had Carly precede him up a wide, curving staircase, his hand on her bare shoulder, her slip left behind in the front hall. Carly could still taste the salty, mushroom flavor of Adam's semen on her tongue and she could still feel the imprint of his hand on both cheeks. Despite her embarrassment at having proven disobedient in the face of his direct command, her cunt felt swollen and wet. Having her face slapped had always been a sexual trigger, a fact of which he was probably aware, since it was in her dossier.

On the second floor Adam guided her down a thickly-carpeted hallway. As they walked, Carly caught a glimpse of what must be the master bedroom, a large brass bed on one side, a sitting area on the other, complete with its own stone fireplace.

At the end of the hall Adam had her stop in front of a narrow door. Pulling a key from his pocket, he unlocked the door and pulled it open. Unlike the wide, polished wood stairs leading to the second floor, these were narrow and covered with thin, well-worn carpeting. They led, Carly imagined, to what must have been servants' quarters at one time. Now, she thought with a shiver of nervous but excited anticipation, they must lead to Adam's dungeon.

When they got to the top of the stairs, Carly expected to see the typical setup she was used to from the BDSM clubs—with the requisite St. Andrew's Cross, whipping posts, chains hanging from the ceiling, manacles imbedded in the walls, bondage tables, and plenty of whips and floggers either hung along the walls or in their own special racks.

Instead, the space they entered looked more like a den or game room, with large armchairs and a sofa set around what looked like a long, wide storage chest, the top covered with a fitted leather pad. There was a bookshelf against one wall, and a globe resting on a marble pedestal beside one of the armchairs. Against the far wall stood a cabinet with two columns of drawers. Beside it was a tall wardrobe, its double doors closed. A grandfather clock stood in the corner, its brass pendulum swinging slowly. There was even a pool table in a corner of the large room, covered in kelly-green felt.

Carly scanned the walls, looking for the door that would lead to the actual dungeon when Adam said, "Welcome to my dungeon. You'll be spending quite a lot of time here over the next thirty days."

She nearly blurted out her questioning surprise, catching herself just in time as she recalled his rule that she must ask permission before speaking. "Excuse me, Sir. May I speak?"

"No."

Carly drew in a breath and hiccupped in her effort to stop herself from giving voice to the words that had already formed at her lips.

Adam was looking at her, his eyes narrowed. "You were anticipating that I would say yes. Never anticipate, Carly. When you ask for something, you make damn sure I approve, get it?"

"Yes, Sir," Carly replied, embarrassed.

"You're wondering where the toys are—I can see it in your face." He waved a hand around the large room. "They're all here, just not necessarily in evidence. You'll get to know every inch of this space before I'm done with you. I plan to get my money's worth, slave girl. When you leave here, you will have earned your keep, and then some."

His words hung heavy between them, balanced between a promise and a threat, and for the first time since this stranger had bid on her, Carly felt a whisper of fear brush its way through her, making her shiver. What if he took her too far? It wasn't as if she could just walk out. Was she really up for this? Could she handle whatever this man had in store for her?

Adam's smile was slow, at once sensual and cruel as he moved his eyes appraisingly over her naked body. "It's late, and you're waiting for your punishment." He pointed toward the padded chest. "I want you to crouch on the cock box. Disobedient slave girls need a good, hard spanking to remind them of their place."

Cock box? What the hell was that? Was the chest filled with dildos? Carly didn't dare ask. She approached the chest, her lower lip caught in her teeth. Upon closer inspection she saw that there were holes drilled into the wood along the sides of the chest near one end.

Air holes? *Cock box.* Were those holes for…? Carly didn't allow herself to complete the thought.

"Get on your hands and knees, ass in the air," Adam said. "I don't want a sound from you, not a peep. And don't forget—this is a punishment. I'll stop when I'm done, not when you think I should be done, is that understood?"

"Yes, Sir," Carly whispered. She assumed the position on top of the chest, which was wide enough to allow her to balance comfortably on her hands and knees. She felt Adam's hand on her back, guiding her shoulders downward until they were touching the padded wood, forcing the target of her ass up high and clearly exposing her shaven cunt at the same time. Turning her head, she rested her cheek against the cool, soft leather.

She jumped a little when she felt his hand on her lower back. "Not that I expect you'll need it right now, but this is as good a time as any to give you your safeword. Since I bought you at auction, the word will be *auction*. I warn you now, don't use your safeword lightly. It's an absolute last resort, to be used only when you don't feel you can take another second of whatever is happening to you." His hand moved over her ass, making her skin tingle.

"I'm confident you understand the seriousness of using the safeword, and I like to think I pay enough attention to my sub's reactions and responses that it will never be necessary for you to use it. But we are just getting to know one another, and this situation, by definition, demands your immediate trust without allowing us the time to get there naturally." He ran his finger lightly along the cleft between her cheeks. "If you use the word, all action will cease. If I later determine you used it only because you were afraid or resistant, your punishment will be swift and absolute. Are we quite clear?"

"Yes, Sir," Carly replied, committing the word to memory. She, too, hoped she would never have to use it.

"Now we'll get on with tonight's punishment," Adam continued. "No ropes, no chains. You will remain in position and take what you deserve."

Carly wasn't afraid she wouldn't be able to take the pain—she had a high tolerance for pain, especially when it was in an erotic context. She could handle a single tail whip and the cane—surely the spanking would be a piece of cake by comparison. She was more afraid she wouldn't comport herself with "proper slave decorum", as the auction house trainers had drummed into her. She had never been good at keeping quiet or still, and always welcomed restraints that would take the decision and need for self-control away from her. Staying still and quiet, she knew, would be the real test.

She had to prove she was more than just a masochist out for thrills. She had to show Adam she was an obedient and submissive sex slave, even though in her heart of hearts she had no idea if this were true.

As much as she had enjoyed the BDSM play at the clubs and the games she'd engaged in with her boyfriends, her training at the auction house made it crystal clear she had little idea what a Master/slave relationship really entailed. It was money that had motivated her to sign up for this, and she'd fervently hoped as the week of training progressed that she had what it took to convince someone she was the real deal.

The trainers must have seen something in her, because they'd allowed her to complete the course and be a part of the auction. One woman named Patty had been thrown out of the program after the third day, once it became clear she had signed up solely because of the lure of the money. Patty had trouble with even the mildest whipping, and had balked during the humiliation, flat out refusing a direct command.

Master Franklin had warned them some Masters used verbal and physical humiliation training as a means of control, and the slave girls needed to be prepared for whatever came their way. But when he'd ordered Patty to squat in front of them all and pee on some newspapers, it had been too much for her. Mistress Audrey had escorted her from the training dungeon, and that was the last Carly had seen of Patty.

Though she'd misrepresented her experience level to the trainers, Carly had handled and endured everything thrown her way, determined to get through it. She'd been prepared to go with any of the men who bid on her, even if they were old, fat and smelly. She knew she was incredibly lucky that Adam Wise had wanted her. He was handsome, sexy, and based on how he'd touched her in the car, he definitely knew his way around a woman.

The first swat was sudden and hard, a solid thwack against both cheeks. Carly bit back on her grunt of surprise and gripped the overhanging lip of the chest lid to steady herself. The second swat was just as hard, catching her upper thighs, the sting bringing tears to her eyes. He began to hit her in a steady rhythm, though she was never quite sure where the blows would land. It wasn't long before every inch of her ass and the backs of her thighs were on fire, and it was all she could do to keep the whimpers from getting past her clenched teeth.

She tried to ease herself into the pain the way the trainers had taught her, to let herself glide and flow with it, to become one with it, but she was too keyed up, and too nervous in this new environment to move into that headspace. She realized she was gripping the padded wood so hard her fingers were spasming. Her body was rigid with the effort to stay still as blow after blow pounded through her frame.

The skin on her ass and thighs felt flayed and bruised, and still he smacked her, each blow stinging increasingly tender skin. Adam began to focus on one spot, just where her left thigh met her ass cheek, smacking it over and over until Carly thought it might burst into actual flame. Tears were flying from the corners of her eyes and it was too much, too much. Her mouth flew open, the rush of pain pushing past her lips.

"Noooooooooo!" she wailed. Falling to her side, she crouched on the padded chest, curling tight as she twisted away from Adam's relentless palm. She was gasping, trying to get the breath to speak, to beg, to apologize, but all she managed to say was, "No, no, no, no…"

Strong arms encircled her, lifting her into the air. She realized Adam had settled with her on the sofa.

Again she tried to speak, but only whimpers escaped between shuddering breaths. Carly realized she was trembling. Without realizing what she was doing, she burrowed her head against Adam's chest. Her face hidden, she waited for his rebuke, half expecting him to push her from his lap and let her tumble to the floor.

Instead he just held her, saying nothing, letting her remain curled in his strong arms. Carly realized suddenly that she was exhausted. The last night in the slave quarters she'd barely slept. Nervous and excited about auction day, she and the other slave girls had stayed up late whispering, though each was confined to her own bed, chained by wrists and ankles to the bedstead to get them used to sleeping in shackles.

Eventually one girl after the other had drifted off, but Carly had remained awake, watching the sky turn from black to gray to lavender and gold as the dawn spilled through the high windows of their dormitory. Nervous energy had kept her wide-eyed and edgy all day and through the auction, but now she found herself bone-weary.

It felt good to be in someone's arms, even if it was a man who regarded her solely as a purchased piece of ass. It had been a long time since she'd been held. And though that was by choice, it hadn't made it any less lonely.

Just a little longer, she silently begged the stranger cradling her so gently. Her ass and thighs still throbbed with pain and she knew she'd be bruised tomorrow, but right now she felt so good, cocooned safe and small in his arms. *Just a little longer...*

~*~

Adam stared down at the sleeping girl in his arms, not sure what to think or how to feel. He knew he shouldn't have picked her up—they weren't lovers, and she was being punished, after all. He had needed to set a precedent for their future interactions, and he had meant to be stern and clear. Instead, at the first wail he'd stopped the punishment and lifted her into his arms as if she were a child, instead of a hired sex slave.

Still, he told himself, it was only her first night. She had clearly been nervous and exhausted. The real training could begin in the morning.

To Carly's credit, she had taken quite a rough spanking. He'd expected her to balk or cry out sooner than she had. She could take a lot of pain. That was a good thing, as he very much liked to dish it out. The sadist in him thrilled to the power and the passion of taking control of another person—of leading them to the limits of their endurance and then giving just enough push to send them over the edge.

Pain wasn't the only means by which he did this—there were many ways to control and use a willing sub, but it was certainly the most direct and immediate way. And there was nothing like a good, hard spanking, that intimate connection of skin on skin, to take the measure of a masochist's willingness and ability to suffer.

Adam probably could have found a willing sub by advertising on one of the BDSM sites, but they would have arrived with all their emotional baggage and expectations, not to mention who knew what diseases. No, much better to buy what he wanted and get just exactly what he paid for, and nothing more. There was no pretext or pretense. He would enjoy the process of claiming Carly's body and mind, but he had no interest whatsoever in her heart.

The setup was ideal and well worth the money he'd spent. For the month he had this girl in his power, he would use her in ways he might not dare with a lover. He would take her to the very limits of her tolerance, testing her and pushing her, without having to worry or care what she thought of him. He had carte blanche, short of drawing blood, which held no interest for him anyway. He could give free rein to all his darkest, dirtiest fantasies, and she would take it, all of it, or forfeit the money that was undoubtedly her sole motivation for being there. When the month was over, he'd send her on her way.

Neat. Clean. Simple.

The clock began to chime the midnight hour. Carly stirred and nuzzled against Adam's chest. After a moment her deep, slow breathing resumed. Adam shook her shoulder gently. "Hey. Wake up."

Carly lifted her head suddenly, her eyes flying open. "Oh!" As he let her go, she rolled from his lap to the carpet and knelt, her head touching the ground. "I'm sorry, Sir! I'm very sorry. I don't know what happened. I didn't mean to—"

"Enough." Adam stood, stepping away from her. "I don't like whining or excuses. And stop speaking when you haven't been spoken to. Obviously your memory isn't too good. You've already forgotten the rules. Tomorrow I'll have you write them down until you know them by heart, and if you forget again, your punishment will be severe. Do I make myself clear?"

She looked up at him with wide eyes. "Yes, Sir," she breathed. "I—yes, Sir."

"Good." Adam turned on his heel and headed for the stairs. "Come on. It's time for bed." He turned back, watching her approach him. Again he had her go first down the stairs, keeping his hand on her shoulder to guide her. Her ass was still bright red and he knew it had to hurt. He noticed the two small dimples indenting the flesh just over her cheeks and was charmed in spite of himself.

At the bottom of the stairs he took the lead, moving toward his bedroom. Once inside, he turned to her. "Do you need to pee?"

"Yes, Sir."

Adam pointed toward the master bath and Carly went into it. He followed her, watching as she sat on the toilet. He could see by the blush moving over her skin and the way she averted her eyes that she was embarrassed to pee in front of him, which amused him. This girl blushed so easily, it was almost hard to believe she was a paid professional.

When she was done, he allowed her to wash her hands and face. "Are you hungry?" he asked. She shook her head. He showed her the toothbrush he had bought for her and let her brush her teeth. When she was done, he said, "Pull back my bedding and then wait for me on the floor beside the bed. Kneel up, knees spread, back arched, arms behind your head."

Adam used the toilet and washed up, watching her in the mirror as he did so. She was kneeling as instructed. Her profile was to him, the curve of her pretty breasts lifted by her position. Her nipples jutted out, as if begging for clamps. Her arms were lean and muscular. He wondered how long she could keep a position like that, with her fingers laced behind her neck, her back arched. She was tired, he knew that. What better time to test both her endurance and her obedience?

Adam returned to the bedroom and took off his clothing, loosely folding them on the brass clothing rack he kept for the purpose. Naked, he sat down on the bed. "Turn to face me. Stay in that position." He watched as Carly shifted. She had her eyes down and was again worrying her lower lip. Adam said nothing, though he would correct that first thing tomorrow.

Reaching down, he grabbed hold of one nipple. He felt it engorging against his fingers. He squeezed it and twisted. Carly's nostrils flared but she kept silent. Letting go, he slapped her breast lightly, enjoying the jiggle of her flesh. Stretching out on the sheets, Adam reached again for Carly, this time tweaking and twisting the other nipple until a tiny whimper escaped her pretty lips. He reached for his cock, lazily stroking it without any real intention to jerk off.

It felt good to stretch out. It had been a long day, with him wrapping up some business at his firm in order to clear the next few weeks, and then dinner with some associates before the auction that evening. Now he had his prize, but he would take his time with her.

In his twenties and early thirties, he knew he would have been all over her, eager as a little boy in a candy store. But time and experience had taught him patience. Patience always yielded far better rewards than leaping without looking.

He thought again about Carly's orgasm in the car—she was very responsive but seemed to lack much control. It would be fun to teach her that control along with all the other delicious tortures he had planned. The cock box, the water chamber, the torture table... Adam's cock throbbed with anticipation.

Carly's arms had begun to tremble slightly, but she maintained her position, her eyes still downcast. Adam rolled onto his side, peering down between her spread knees. She had a pretty cunt. It would look lovely clamped and spread, as he fucked her with various toys, his fingers and finally, once she'd earned it, his cock.

The girl was worrying her lower lip again, and her arms were now shaking. Taking pity on her, Adam said, "You may lower your arms. Under the bed you'll find a plastic bin. Inside is your coverlet and pillow. You will sleep at the foot of my bed. You will not get out of the bed without my express permission. Got it?"

"Yes, sir." She lowered her arms, hugging herself as she massaged her fatigued muscles. She reached beneath the bed and pulled out the bin. She climbed onto the bed and for a moment Adam almost told her to lie next to him—it would feel good to have someone fall asleep in his arms, resting her head on his chest. Quickly he shook the idea aside, watching as the girl lay down at his feet, stretching out beneath the light coverlet and resting her head on the pillow.

Reaching for the lamp, he flicked it off. He had expected to stay awake for a while, his mind filled with ideas about what he was going to do to this naked slave girl lying so submissively at his feet. But his eyes closed of their own accord and he felt the tug of sleep pulling him under almost before he could mumble, "Good night, Carly."

"Good night, Sir."

Chapter 4

After a week spent on a hard cot with chains on her ankles and wrists, sleeping at the foot of Adam's incredibly comfortable bed had felt like sleeping in a soft, warm cocoon of pure comfort. Carly had lain awake for a while listening to the quiet, steady rumble of Adam's snore. He, it seemed, had fallen asleep almost as soon as his head hit the pillow. Carly was glad of this, as it gave her time to think and relax in peace.

She had planned to review the evening in her mind, going over every detail, marking what she needed to correct and improve, mulling over the rush of events since the auctioneer had slammed down his gavel. But apparently she'd been as tired as her temporary Master, because now as she opened her eyes, she saw through the large bay windows on the east side of Adam's huge bedroom that it was morning. The play of the rising sun's light behind the trees made them look as if they were on fire, but a green, glittering fire, tinged with gold on the edges.

Adam stirred, mumbling something in his sleep and turning from his side to his back. Was it too early to wake him? Carly needed to pee, but remembered his rules. She didn't want to wake him to ask permission. The trainers had drummed into her the paramount rule that a Master's comfort must come first. Then she remembered one of the rules he'd outlined: *I expect to be awakened by your mouth on my cock.*

Her mind flashed back to the night before, to kneeling on the cold marble, Adam's cock down her throat, his fingers tangled in her hair. Though Carly had thought herself a reasonably accomplished cocksucker prior to the week's training at the auction house, the hours she'd spent with Master Franklin's cock in her mouth had definitely helped to hone her skills. Mistress Audrey's constant direction, quirt in hand to provide correction, had spurred on Carly's efforts, as eager to avoid the sting of the quirt as to please her Master.

Where Master Franklin's cock was long and thin, with a bent toward the left, Adam's was shorter but thick, straight as a rod and hard as steel. He smelled good, too, like sandalwood with a splash of masculine musk that had made her cunt wet even before her lips had closed over the fat head of his shaft.

Cautiously, Carly lifted her head, looking at the sleeping man above her. His dark hair, which had been neatly combed back the night before, was tousled, curling against his neck and flopping forward over his eyes. He looked younger in sleep, thick eyelashes brushing his cheeks, his mouth slack. She found herself wondering what it would be like to kiss that mouth...

Stop it, she admonished herself. *He's not your lover.*

He stirred again, turning his head from the sunlight now streaming in through the window and throwing one arm over his face. He was going to wake soon—she needed to act now, to obey the first rule of the morning.

Pushing aside her coverlet, Carly scooted up alongside the sleeping man and plucked at the sheets that covered his body. She drew them down only far enough to expose his cock and balls, taking a few seconds to admire his morning erection before lowering herself to taste him.

She licked the soft, spongy head of his cock and down the shaft. A long, thick vein on the underside of his cock stood in relief beneath the taut skin. She ran her tongue along it, feeling the throbbing pulse of his blood. Reaching for his balls, she caught the furred sac in a light embrace with her fingers, enjoying the heft and warmth of them. With a last glance at his face, which was still in sleepy repose, she lowered her mouth over his cock, tasting the light, salty tang as she licked her way downward.

Adam's hand came to rest on the back of her head, though otherwise he remained still. Carly went to work, intent on making him come quickly, her bladder urging her on. Still, she knew from her training and her own life experience that it wouldn't do to make him feel rushed. *Your discomfort is secondary to your Master's pleasure.* Master Franklin's words echoed in her head, reminding her to slow down. She alternated between a deep-throated suckle and feather-light tongue teasing that made him shudder and arch upward for more.

The hand resting on the back of her head came alive suddenly, his fingers twisting in her hair and pulling hard as he pressed her downward onto his shaft. Sudden hot bursts of his creamy come spurted at the back of her throat, sliding down before she even had a chance to swallow. He thrust against her with a primal grunt and then held her in place for several seconds, his cock still hard and hot in her mouth, the head lodged in her throat making it difficult to breathe.

Finally he let her go, his fingers uncoiling from her hair, his muscles going slack against the bed. Cautiously Carly lifted her head, letting his spent shaft fall from her mouth. Adam's eyes were closed, his lips lightly parted. His chest was rising and falling in a deep, steady rhythm.

Shit, had he fallen asleep again? What was she supposed to do now? She really had to pee. Did she dare wake him?

Carly stared at the sleeping man for several long moments, trying to figure out what to do. Finally she sidled up beside him and whispered, "Please, Sir. May I use the toilet?"

There was no response, save for the steady rise and fall of his breathing.

Carly bit her lower lip, wondering if she should ask again, or just lie down and be quiet until he woke. It wouldn't do to piss him off first thing in the morning. Did she dare slip quietly out of the bed, pee, and then hurry back, with him none the wiser?

But what if her movement woke him? Or worse, he woke up while she was in the bathroom! She couldn't risk it. With a sigh, she started to lie down beside him, then caught herself and scooted back down to the foot of the bed. Just as her head touched her pillow, Adam said, "Yes. You may use the toilet and then come back for your mark."

Carly lifted her head to look at him. Adam had hoisted himself onto his elbows, his mouth lifted in a sardonic smile. He'd been testing her! Thank god she hadn't given in to her aching bladder.

Quickly she slipped from the bed and hurried to the bathroom. After peeing, she washed her hands and face, staring at herself in the mirror. Her hair was a mess, the curls tangled and disheveled, but she didn't even bother to try and do anything, knowing it would be useless until she showered. Her face looked pale in the fluorescent lighting of the bathroom, and she wished she could put on a little makeup before heading back into the bedroom. Where were her things, anyway? Still down in the front hall?

In the mirror Carly saw Adam watching her from the bed and quickly rubbed a hand towel over her face before scurrying back to him. As she reentered the bedroom, he pointed toward the night table. "Open the bottom drawer. There you will find the whip I will use each morning to mark you. This mark is a reminder of my ownership of you during your stay here."

Carly reached for the handle of the drawer and pulled it open. Coiled inside was a braided single tail whip with knots every couple of inches, the leather tapering to thin strips of tassled nylon that Carly knew from experience could pack a powerful sting.

As she reached for the whip, Adam sat upright, swinging his legs over the side of the bed. "Present it to me," he said.

Kneeling up as she'd been taught the week before, Carly balanced the whip handle on her open palms and held it up to Adam.

He took it from her and stood. "Lie over the bed, your feet on the floor, arms over your head. Not a sound."

Carly lifted herself as instructed and closed her eyes, bracing herself for the bite of the whip. The leather tail whistled through the air and landed with a sharp crack across her ass.

"Ah!" Carly screamed.

Adam pulled her upright by her hair and slapped her face. "Bad girl. I said not a sound." Letting go of her hair, he gave her a little push in the direction of the bathroom. "We'll deal with that transgression later. You get into the shower. I'll bring up your bag so you have what need."

Carly had been permitted to pack toiletries, including her own shampoo and conditioner. She had been allowed to bring clothing for when she left the house, as well as her cell phone, though this was only to be used for emergencies, and only with permission.

Her hand on the cheek Adam had slapped, Carly entered the bathroom again, gazing with longing at the huge sunken Jacuzzi bathtub. Maybe one day he'd let her soak in it. For now, she opened the shower stall. It was as big as her entire bathroom in the house she'd rented. There were two showerheads on the ceiling and three more on either side of the stall. The far wall was mirrored, a low tiled bench set against it. It took her a moment to figure out how to turn on the overhead spigots. While the water was warming, she walked back to the mirror over the two sinks and turned around, peering back to see the mark on her ass. A faint smudge of purple bruises from the spanking the night before mottled both cheeks. Overlaying these, a long dark red line ran in a diagonal across her right cheek. She touched the welt, moving her finger along its rise. She felt at once awed and proud as she stared at it. She had taken the mark. Next time she would do better, though. She would contain her scream, now that she knew what to expect.

The water was steaming, and Carly reentered the stall and stood beneath the cascading water, soaking up the delicious heat. She heard Adam coming into the bathroom and a moment later he pulled open the stall door. He held out her mesh shower basket, which contained her shampoo, conditioner, soap cream bar, shaving oil and her two razors. As Carly took them, he said, "Present yourself in the bedroom for inspection when you're done. And be quick about it. I'm hungry."

"Yes, Sir. Thank you."

Carly shampooed her hair and then squirted conditioner in, pulling it through to the ends. She soaped up her body and then took the razor she used for her underarms and labia. Using the shaving oil, she lifted one leg onto the bench, peering into the mirror as she shaved her cunt, taking care to leave the skin perfectly smooth. Taking the heavier duty razor, she shaved her legs after squirting a generous amount of the shaving oil over the skin to keep it soft. Finally she rinsed her hair and turned off the water, mindful of his admonition to hurry.

There was a stack of thick, fluffy white towels on a shelf beside the stall. Carly wound one around her head and used a second one to dry her body. She saw Adam had placed her toiletry bag on the counter beside one of the sinks. The other sink had his razor and toothbrush set in a holder.

As she moved to the mirror, she thought, *this is my sink*, and it made her smile, even though she knew that possession was extremely temporary. She'd lived only once with a man, back in her mid-twenties. They had rented a small apartment together in Brooklyn. The bathroom, which was barely large enough to turn around in, had one sink, which always seemed to be filled with the remnants of Josh's beard after he shaved. Glancing at Adam's sink, she was pleased to note it was spotless.

Using mousse designed to tame curls, she sprayed some on her palm, rubbed her hands together and ran them through her hair. She hoped Adam didn't mind wet hair, as a blow dryer always ended up turning her curls into a fright wig of frizz. She looked around for her makeup bag, but didn't see it. She touched her cheeks, wondering if Adam had purposely held it back, deciding that he must have. At thirty-two, though her skin was clear and unwrinkled, she felt more attractive using the armor of blush, lipstick and mascara. But if her temporary Master didn't want it, so be it.

With a last tug at her curls, Carly left the bathroom and entered the bedroom, where Adam waited in the sitting area. Wearing a yellow silk robe, he sat in a wingback chair beside a large window reading a newspaper. There was a steaming cup of coffee beside him, and the aroma made Carly's mouth water. As she approached him, he folded the paper, setting it down on the small side table as he stood.

"Arms behind your head, legs shoulder-width apart," he said. Carly assumed the position, used to daily inspections from her week of slave training. Adam moved close, running his index finger under her arm. It tickled and she tried hard to stay still, resisting the urge to squirm away. He did the same under her second arm, and then reached down, cupping her mons in his large hand. He ran his fingers lightly over her labia and then stepped back.

Reaching into his robe pocket, he extracted a small, slim flashlight and flicked it on. "Turn around, bend over and grab your ankles. Keep your legs spread wide." Carly stared at the flashlight and swallowed. Though used to being naked in front of others, she didn't like the idea of such an up-close and personal examination of her private parts.

Biting her lip, she turned and bent forward, reaching for her ankles. "Wider," Adam said, smacking her inner thigh with the flashlight. Carly obeyed, feeling awkward and exposed. She felt the heat scalding her cheeks as Adam's fingers again moved over her labia and slid up along the cleft, lightly rimming her asshole. His finger moved over the welt he'd left on her ass and then he smacked her other cheek.

"Good," he said, stepping back. "You pass. Stand up and turn around." As Carly did so, he said, "Are you hungry?"

Carly was starving, she realized, having been too nervous the day before to eat much of anything, and she would kill for a cup of coffee. "Yes, Sir," she replied.

She expected Adam to lead her downstairs, but instead he appeared to be heading toward the bathroom. "I'm going to shower and shave first. You will wait on the bathmat so you can dry me when I get out. Then we'll have some breakfast."

Her stomach growling, Carly cast a wistful glance at the coffee mug he'd left beside his chair and followed him into the bathroom. While Adam showered, she waited dutifully on her knees on the thick bathmat in front of the sinks. When he came out of the shower, she leaned up with a towel, drying his legs, balls and penis while he used a second towel to dry his head and torso. The act had the curious effect of making her feel almost tender toward him, but she pushed these feelings away.

She knelt quietly at his feet while he shaved over his sink. She admired the strong curve of his calf muscles, which were covered with dark, curling hair. His thighs were powerful and his ass was firm. Why did this man have to *buy* a slave? He was gorgeous, wealthy and dominant. He could have had his pick of women with a snap of his fingers. He probably had to fend them off as it was, both vanilla women and those in the scene.

Maybe that was it. He didn't want women hurling themselves at him. He didn't want a love affair. He didn't want an emotional connection. He just wanted a toy—someone to use and then discard when he grew bored. No strings, no complications.

Perfect for me too, Carly staunchly told herself, refusing to give in to the niggling suspicion that she might be lying. *Just perfect.*

~*~

Adam stood at the stove scrambling eggs while the bread was toasting. Carly had almost slipped up, nearly sitting down on one of the kitchen chairs after he'd told her he would get the breakfast. Catching herself in time, she'd knelt instead on the small exercise pad he'd placed on the floor by the table for her. Adam felt the way he did the first morning of a vacation, with all that glorious time stretching ahead of him, everything new and waiting to be explored.

Only this was better than a vacation. Everything he wanted to explore was right here in this kitchen, kneeling obediently behind him, waiting for whatever delightful tortures he could devise. Adam's cock stirred at the thought. He'd pulled on a pair of khaki shorts after his shower, not bothering with underwear or a shirt. Though summer was nearing its end, it was already warm outside, climbing to eighty-four according to the thermometer affixed to the kitchen window, and it wasn't even nine o'clock yet.

He dumped the steaming eggs onto a plate, pulled the toast from the toaster and spread some butter over it. Refilling his cup, he carried it along with the plate to the table.

Though he rarely ate breakfast himself, he took several bites of egg and ate half a piece of toast before turning to Carly, who was watching his every move like a dog waiting to be tossed a scrap. Adding some cream, he took a sip of his coffee, appraising his slave girl over the rim. Her eyes, he realized, were the color of robin's eggs, a rich, pure blue. She glanced submissively down in the face of his gaze.

"You have a choice," he told her. "You can eat from the plate on the floor, mouth only, no utensils. Or I can feed you."

Carly pursed her lips, not quite managing to hide the confused, annoyed expression that flitted over her features. Adam lifted another bite of egg to his mouth, following it with another long sip of coffee.

"Feed me, please, Sir," she finally blurted, actually licking her lips.

Nodding, Adam held out a piece of toast, allowing her take a bite. He scooped up some egg on the fork and let her take it. He continued to feed her until the plate was empty. "Do you like coffee or would you prefer orange juice?"

"Coffee, please," she said quickly. Adam finished what was in his cup and stood, heading toward the pot.

Turning back, he asked, "How do you take it?"

"Cream and three spoons of sugar, please, Sir."

He poured the coffee and added the cream, not quite able to hide his smile as he stirred in the ridiculous amount of sugar. The coffee was steaming hot, and while he planned to hurt her today, accidentally burning her with scalding coffee was not the way he intended to do it. Handing her the cup, he said, "Here. You can hold it. When you're done, wash the dishes and wipe down the counters."

He took up the newspaper, pretending to ignore her as she sipped and then gulped the sweet coffee. When she was done she stood, smoothing her thighs as if she were smoothing the fabric of the skirt that wasn't there. She cleared the dishes and went to the sink. He watched her openly as she cleaned up, again admiring the small dimples over her ass cheeks and the welt that, though fading, was still visible.

When Carly was done, she turned toward Adam, an expectant look on her face. Adam stood. "This morning I was going to begin with a flogging session just to warm you up, but you have an annoying habit that needs breaking. Follow me."

Biting her lower lip, Carly followed him out of the kitchen and up the two flights of stairs to his dungeon. He left her standing in the middle of the room while he went to the cabinet and opened the drawer containing his gag collection. Finding what he was looking for, he removed it from its sterilized container and brought it to his naked slave girl, holding it out for her inspection.

"Do you know what this is?"

Carly stared at it with wide eyes. "No, Sir," she breathed.

"It's called a Whitehead gag. It was originally designed for dentists, the ultimate sadists, for when they want to keep your mouth wide open." He touched her lips. "Open up. I'll show you."

Carly took a step back and Adam glared at her. "I said open your mouth." He spoke sternly, daring her with his eyes to defy him. With obvious reluctance, Carly did as she was told. Adam placed the metal device in her mouth, positioning it behind her front teeth. Slowly he cranked the ratchet on the side of the gag, forcing her mouth wide open before locking it into place.

He massaged his cock through his shorts, toying with the idea of fucking her face, but first things first, he told himself. "Do you know why you're wearing this particular gag, Carly?"

She shook her head, making an ineffectual sound.

"It's because I'm tired of watching you nibble on your lower lip like it was a teething toy. You've been doing it since the second I bought you, despite my telling you repeatedly to stop it. It's a bad habit, and not at all suitable behavior for a sub. I won't have it, do you understand?"

The girl nodded, unable to reply, a miserable expression on her face. Adam continued, "You will wear this while you write your rules. It may be a little awkward but it's perfectly safe."

He led her to the cock box and had her kneel there. He brought over a clipboard with a pad of paper on it and set it, along with a pen, in front of her. Reaching into his shorts pocket, he took out the list of rules he'd typed up on his laptop while she was in the shower and set it beside the clipboard.

"You will write the rules, word for word, until you know them by heart. I'll quiz you afterwards, so make damn sure you memorize them." Carly lifted her hand to her open mouth, about to wipe a string of drool that slipped from the corner.

Adam stopped her, his hand on her wrist. "Un unh," he informed her. "The drool will help you remember, next time you think about biting your lip. Right now you're a drooling, naked object, and nothing more. You are being punished." He let go of her wrist, watching as the drool slid down her chin and onto her breasts. "Now get on with it."

Tears in her pretty eyes, Carly looked at the printed list of rules, took up the pen, and began to write.

Chapter 5

Carly's chin and chest were covered with her own drool and her jaw ached. If he'd just take this horrible contraption off her, she'd never bite her lip again, she swore to herself. She'd written the rules five times and was reasonably sure they were imprinted on her brain. Setting the pen down on the ink-covered page, she sat back on her haunches, looking toward Adam with silent yearning.

He was in the chair across from her, a newspaper in his hands. He seemed engrossed in whatever he was reading. Carly tried to clear her throat, but only succeeded in making a strangled sort of gargling noise. It was enough, however, to make him look up.

"Yes?" he said, folding the paper. "Are you done?"

Carly nodded.

"What's that?" Adam said, lifting his eyebrows. "Speak up, I didn't hear you."

"Eh ir," was the best approximation Carly could manage. *Get this fucking thing off me!* she wanted to scream.

"So, if I remove the dental gag, you will recite the rules for me, in their entirety?"

"Eh, ir," she gargled.

Placing the folded paper on the floor beside his chair, Adam stood and moved around the chest toward her. She leaned up, bending her head so he could unbuckle the gag, but instead she realized he was unzipping his shorts. Pulling out his cock, he took her head in both hands and guided her wide-open mouth over his shaft.

Carly gagged as the rapidly hardening cock poked far back against her throat. He thrust hard, pulling and pushing her head to create friction, while Carly struggled to breathe and swallow. As quickly as he started, however, he stopped, pulling away. He let his shorts fall to the ground and kicked them aside.

Bending down, he released the gag from its open position, allowing Carly to close her aching jaws. Unbuckling the strap, he pulled the gag from her mouth. Reaching for his shorts, he extracted something from the pocket and tossed her a bit of cloth that she realized was a handkerchief. Gratefully Carly wiped away the drool, while working her aching jaw.

"You've memorized the rules?" Adam asked as he watched her wiping herself.

"Yes, Sir," Carly replied, unable to look away from the erect cock bobbing near her face.

"I thought about just having you recite them, but decided that would be too easy. A properly trained slave should be able to handle external stimuli while performing whatever task is assigned to her. I've decided this stimulus will be sexual in nature."

Carly didn't reply, as there had been no direct question, but her mind and body were instantly buzzing with the possibilities. What would it be like to feel that hard, thick cock filling her? Would she be able to focus enough to say her lines?

Adam apparently had something else in mind however, as he led her to a freestanding metal frame on the far side of the room that she realized she'd taken for a coat rack the night before. This morning nylon cuffs with Velcro closures were hanging from the top bar. Beneath it sat a low, wide stool covered in faded silk upholstery. Carly stood with her arms wrapped around her torso while she watched Adam, hardly daring to speculate what came next.

Reaching for the top bar, he released some kind of spring, which allowed him to lower the bar between the vertical rods that held it in place. She imagined he would have her sit on the stool, her wrists cuffed overhead, but instead Adam pointed toward the stool. "Lie face up on the stool so your lower back is straddling it. I'm going to lift your legs and strap your ankles to the bar."

Carly tried to obey, feeling awkward and uncertain as she lay back on the stool. Grasping her ankles and pulling her legs upward, Adam secured them into the cuffs and then hoisted the bar up again. The position wasn't precisely uncomfortable, as her neck and shoulders rested securely on the stool, but the position left her feeling very vulnerable.

Leaving her alone, he returned a moment later with a hank of rope, which he wound around her wrists, forcing her hands down to her chest, where they rested as if in prayer between her breasts. As it always did, the feel of rope against her skin sent shivers of warm, wet desire moving through Carly's loins.

Leaving her yet again, Adam came back with a black pair of clover clamps, which he held so she could see. Pinching her nipple between thumb and forefinger, he opened one of the clips and let the rubber-tipped metal pincher close over the distended nipple.

Gripping the other nipple, Adam closed the second pincher over the hard nubbin. Carly winced and let out a breath as she struggled to adjust to the pulse of pain in her breasts. Her nipples throbbed in unison in the tight grip of the clover clamps. A tug on the chain between them made her moan in pain as it caused the clips to tighten even more against her sensitive nipples.

Letting the chain drop, Adam pushed at the ankle cuffs that secured her to the bar overhead, forcing her legs wider to fully expose her cunt. In spite of her predicament and her pain, or partially because of them, she felt her labia swelling in anticipation of his touch. She flashed back to the night before, to the sensual, dominant way he'd taken her over in the car, wresting a powerful orgasm from her that had left her stunned.

The sudden, sharp smack to her spread labia pulled a scream of startled surprise from Carly's lips. This was followed by a moan as Adam licked his finger and pushed it inside her, curling it in a way that sent a shudder of need through Carly's frame as he grazed her clit with his palm.

The rope, the clamps, the stroke of his fingers all combined into a powerful erotic sensation that made Carly begin to pant. From her position, she could see no higher than Adam's crotch, where his erection bobbed so close to her face that if she strained she could have licked the shaft. Not that she dared.

"Go on, slave. Recite the rules."

The rules, the rules. What rules? Jesus god, that feels so good. He smells so good. My nipples hurt.

Another smack against Carly's spread cunt, harder than the first, ripped through her nerve endings, making her gasp in pain.

The rules! Say them!

"I will not sit on any furniture," she began haltingly, and then remembered the rest, "without express permission or direction, oh!" He was doing that amazing thing again with his hand that he'd done in the car.

Concentrate, concentrate.

Taking a deep breath, she willed her brain to reconnect, her vocal chords to function, her mouth to form the words.

"I will ask..." She groaned and gasped as he stroked her toward orgasm. A sharp slap elicited another cry.

"Focus," Adam admonished from above.

"I will ask," Carly continued breathlessly, "for permission to eat, oh, oooo..." His fingers were doing an erotic dance over her labia and sliding into her wetness. The pain in her nipples had eased to a dull throb. "Drink, sleep, use the toilet, shower, speak and, oh! Oh, oh, oh!"

"And what, Carly? And what? Tell me."

The blood was rushing in her ears and pounding in her temples. *And what? What was next? Oh god, oh fuck, oh god...* His palm ground against her clit, his fingers moving inside her like a cock. He was standing close, so close his erection brushed against her body. She could smell his musk and her own desire, the scents mingling like an aphrodisiac in the air.

A rush of pleasure so fierce it could have been pain hurtled through her body, making her jerk and writhe in her bonds. "Oh, oh, god, oh, please, I—"

"Tell me," he urged, his voice throaty and low. "Tell me."

Carly's head lifted, her muscles contorting in her effort to close her legs against the onslaught of Adam's relentless fingers. She tried to override the intense sensations that had caused her brain to short-circuit. It was too much, too much. If she could just remember the rest of the rule maybe he would stop, and she could catch her breath, somehow regain some semblance of composure, say the words he demanded from her.

Her body still in the throes of ecstasy, she finally managed to get her brain to spew out the words, hoping she'd remember the ending before she fainted from his touch: *I will ask permission to eat, drink, sleep, use the toilet, shower, speak and...* "To orgasm!" she shouted, jerking in her restraints.

Finally his hand fell away. She hung upside down, trembling, her skin covered in a sheen of sweat, her cunt throbbing. Adam knelt down in front of her, his mouth lifted in a sardonic grin, his eyebrows lifted.

Oh, shit.

"What just happened, Carly?"

He was going to make her say it, adding insult to her injury.

Carly closed her eyes, but forced herself to speak. "I came without permission, Sir."

"That's right, Carly. You did. What happens to slave girls who break the rules?"

"They get punished, Sir."

He nodded. "They do."

Reaching for the nipple clamps, he released them in tandem.

Carly screamed.

~*~

As Adam let the girl down from the bar, his impulse was to take her into his arms and suckle away the pain at her nipples. He was not an impulsive man, he reminded himself, and she was not his lover.

He could see the tears in her eyes and the sheen of sweat on her flushed skin, but beyond those uncontrollable physical reactions, who knew what was real? He wanted to believe the explosive orgasm he'd seemed to pull from her was authentic, but well knew women's ability to fake it, even supposed slave girls.

She swayed as he helped her to stand, dizzy from the blood rushing away from her head. Adam reached to steady her, and then pressed at her shoulder. "Kneel and thank me," he ordered the purchased slave, pointing toward his bare feet. Dutifully the girl dropped to her knees. Her lips were soft as they fluttered over his skin.

"We clearly have a lot of work to do in terms of teaching you to focus," he said to the top of her head as the girl continued to kiss his feet. "You barely got through the second rule." Adam smiled in spite of himself as he said this. If she had been faking, she deserved an Oscar. "You'll recite the rules for me later. Right now I have a few things to attend to. This will be an excellent time for you to do your morning chores."

He led her downstairs to the master bedroom and retrieved the stiletto heels he had bought for whatever slave girl he brought home. Glancing now at Carly's feet, he thought the shoes might be a little big, but they would do.

"You will wear these for all your chores," he informed her. Reaching into the drawer he'd set aside for the other items he'd purchased in anticipation of a slave girl's arrival, Adam pulled out the hobbling cuffs and the outfit she would wear while cleaning.

"Put this on." He handed her the bustier and white lacey French maid's apron, smiling as he watched her struggle into the tight-fitting outfit. The bustier forced her breast together, the top halves spilling lusciously over the bone-stayed satin. It fit tight, tighter than he knew was comfortable, but as long as she could breathe, she should be fine. The apron accentuated her slender waist, while hiding little of her smooth, bare body beneath it. She stepped into the high heels, wobbling slightly as he knelt to attach the ankle cuffs with the hobbling chain between them.

"Walk toward the bathroom and back to me," he instructed Carly. She looked incredibly sexy in the outfit as she took careful, mincing steps toward the bathroom, her gait limited by the chain between her ankles, as was the intention. She had tied the apron's sash in a floppy bow behind her, the loops of which hung over her shapely ass as she walked.

When she returned to him, Adam instructed Carly on how he required the bed made, watching her execute a hospital corner and smooth the sheets just so before showing her how he liked his pillows. "You'll find fresh sheets in the linen closet," he informed her as he pulled away her handiwork, tossing the bedding onto the floor. "I like the sheets changed every two days. Today is a changing day."

"Yes, Sir."

He took her to the bathroom, showing her the hamper for the soiled sheets, the linen closet and where the cleaning supplies were kept. "You will clean out the shower and the Jacuzzi if it's been used. You will wash down the sinks and counters, make sure the towels are fresh and properly folded, clean the mirrors, scour the toilet, wipe down the baseboards and mop the floor. When you think everything is done to my satisfaction, you will press this button here." He showed her the intercom that was set into the wall above the light switch.

"You will wait in the bedroom at attention, arms behind your back, legs spread as far as the chains will allow, until I come to you. You will accompany me during my inspection, and if your work passes muster, all to the good. If not, well..." He shrugged. "Take all the time you need," he added. "It had better be done right."

Adam savored the flash of fear that moved through her pretty blue eyes, his cock swelling at the thought of the delicious punishments he had already devised when she failed to satisfy him, as she invariably would.

"Are we quite clear on this?"

"Yes, Sir."

Adam left her looking through the linen closet for the bedding she would need and headed down to his study. Once seated behind his desk, he logged on to his computer and answered several emails. He started to open the feasibility study file one of his vice presidents had prepared, but instead found himself reaching for the *Erotica Auctions* contract, spreading it flat on his desk and turning to the second page to examine Carly's signature.

Carly Abrams

Her handwriting was clear, the slant slightly to the right, the press of her pen confident and flowing. She was beautiful, sexually responsive, obviously masochistic, possibly submissive. What else did he know about her? Damn little, other than she was willing to sell herself for a few dollars.

Well, not a few, he conceded, though he wasn't sure what percentage of the amount he'd bid for her actually went into her pocket, and what percentage the auction house kept for themselves. Still, it had to be enough to give up whatever you were doing for a month, enough to sell yourself to a man you'd never met. What kind of employer would allow you to take a month-long leave of absence?

Maybe she was independently wealthy, a trust fund baby with more money than sense — overeducated and overindulged. Somehow he doubted this. More likely, she was a checkout clerk at a supermarket or the assistant manager of a hardware store — definitely not the sort of woman who moved in his social circles.

Even if she'd finagled time off from her menial job, if she were involved with someone, especially someone dominant, how could that man allow her to sell herself the way she had? Adam barely allowed himself to acknowledge the satisfaction he felt to realize the odds were excellent that she was unattached.

What do you care?

"I don't," he said aloud, turning toward his computer screen. "Just curious." He typed in Carly's name to see what would come up. A few Twitter and Facebook accounts, a massage therapist in Vermont, none of them his Carly, as far as he could tell.

He closed the browser and turned away from the screen, annoyed with himself. Who cared what the purchased piece of ass did on her own time? Carly was a toy—an expendable, temporary diversion. Nothing more.

Adam clicked open the reports he'd saved onto his desktop, determined to focus. He was immersed in the data when the intercom buzzed. He glanced at his watch—thirty-five minutes. Certainly enough time to complete her assigned tasks, though with her ankles chained and her feet shod in high heels, it would have taken longer to get it all done.

When he arrived upstairs, Carly was standing beside the bed, arms behind her back, breasts thrust out, legs spread, the chain taut between them. She'd knotted her hair at the nape of her neck and wispy tendrils escaped over her forehead and ears. Her lacy apron, he noticed, was wet, the fabric clinging to her thighs.

Briefly Adam fantasized about bending her over the bed and fucking her from behind. It was in the contract—he could fuck her both vaginally and anally as often as he liked. He licked his lips at the thought of pushing her down and pressing his erection between her ass cheeks or into the snug embrace of her wet cunt. Why hadn't he fucked her yet?

Because she hasn't earned it, he told himself. She had yet to properly and completely obey him. A proper slave girl only got fucked as a reward.

Pretending to ignore her, he lifted the quilt and inspected her attention to detail. The corners were neatly tucked, the bedding smooth. The pillows were properly plumped and arranged. So far, so good.

Looping a finger through the O ring at the center of her collar, he led Carly into the bathroom, moving slowly so she could keep up in her chains. While she waited, he inspected the shower, the mirrors, the counters and the floor. He looked into the toilet, and then lifted the seat. Taking a cotton swab from the drawer where he kept them, he ran the tip under the inner rim of the toilet bowl and lifted it for Carly to see.

Her eyes widened in dismay. She started to say something but Adam silenced her with an upheld hand. "Not a word. I didn't ask you a question."

He moved closer to her, waving the soiled swab near her face. "I was told you were trained in service. Did no one teach you to clean beneath the rim of a toilet bowl?"

"I'm sorry, Sir," she said breathlessly. "I thought I had—"

"Not good enough," he interrupted, affecting a stern expression, though in fact he was delighted with this legitimate reason to punish the girl. "Tomorrow you will do better."

Crouching in front of her, Adam removed the hobbling cuffs. "Step out of the shoes," he said, taking those as well. Pointing to her cleaning outfit, he added, "Take off those things and hang them to dry." He motioned toward one of the towel hooks near the Jacuzzi.

"Please, Sir, may I speak?"

"Yes. What is it?"

"May I use the toilet?"

Adam toyed for a moment with the idea of denying her, but decided against it. That sort of play could wait for the water chamber. "Yes, but be quick about it." He headed toward the bedroom, turning back at the bathroom door. "I'll be waiting for you in the dungeon. I'm looking forward to trying out my new candles. The wax burns especially hot."

Chapter 6

Carly hung the wet things on a hook. She sat on the toilet, glad he wasn't watching her this time, as she had to move her bowels as well as pee. A tumble of emotions was churning through her, leaving her almost breathless with confusion.

She'd been so sure she'd done a spectacular cleaning job and had been looking forward to his approval. The bed was flawlessly made, every surface in the bathroom sparkled, the towels were neatly folded and all the cleaning supplies were stored where she'd found them. *Finally*, she had thought, *I've done something he won't be able to find fault with!*

And then he had. Frustration with herself, anger with Adam for no doubt setting her up, chagrin that she hadn't seen it coming — these feelings warred with the constant sexual excitement and anticipation that had settled over her like a net since the moment she'd stood on the auction stage, her eyes locking with the man who had ended up taking her home.

Carly wiped herself and flushed, quickly washing her hands in the sink she already regarded as "hers" after just one day. One day! She hadn't even been in Adam's house for twenty-four hours, and already he'd packed more into the experience than she'd had in a month of Sundays. Would she really be able to endure another twenty-nine days of this kind of constant stimulation? Would Adam? It was the weekend, after all, she reminded herself. It was possible he would work during the week, and what would she do while he was gone?

Stop anticipating.

The trainers had tried to teach the girls about living in the moment, about accepting what was given them by their Masters, and not attempting to anticipate or control events. "Your place and your duty are to serve your Master," Mistress Audrey had told them when they first began the training and many more times over the course of the week. "You do this by obeying, to the letter, his every dictate and command. It isn't about your pleasure or your pain. It's about what pleases *him*. Remember that, and you will be a good slave. Forget it at your peril."

Carly hurried out of the room toward the dungeon stairs, her stomach in a nervous flutter of anticipation. Adam stood near a leather recliner. Beside the recliner was a table upon which sat three large, fat candles, the wicks already lit. In addition to the candles were what looked like two very large pairs of scissors, but instead of pointed tips, each end was covered in an oval of dark pink rubber. The ovals fit flat against one another when the scissors were closed. There was also a vibrating wand, its large, round head already shiny with lubricant. Finally there was a black sleep mask.

Adam pointed to the recliner. "Sit here and I'll strap you in."

Carly saw no straps, but did as she was told. Adam pressed a lever on the side of the chair, causing it to slide back so her body was now parallel to the floor. At the same time, the foot rest section of the chair split apart, forcing Carly's legs wide open. Reaching beneath the chair, Adam lifted leather straps over each of Carly's ankles, securing them. He did the same at her thighs.

"Arms over your head," he ordered, pulling additional straps from the top of the recliner, which he used to bind her wrists together overhead. He picked up a pair of the ominous scissors. "Do you know what these are?"

"No, Sir," Carly whispered, though she was afraid she could guess.

"They're labia clamps. You'll be wearing these throughout the punishment. While not especially painful, they do leave a lovely mark." He reached between her legs, gripping her left outer labia in sure fingers. He opened the first pair of scissors and closed the rubber ovals tight over her flesh.

When Carly winced, Adam smiled cruelly. "Just think of it as erotic discomfort," he said, as he looped a strap through the scissors handle and secured it to the chair. "That might it make it easier to bear."

He did the same thing on the other side, forcing her cunt wide open, her labia caught in the tight, rubber grip of the clamps. He was right—the clamps didn't precisely hurt, but the pressure was intense, and the position fully exposed her already throbbing clit. Even the slightest movement exerted an additional pull on her labia that she realized could cause the so-called erotic discomfort to rapidly edge into pain.

Carly turned her head, drawn to the burning candles, each of which already had a pool of hot, melted wax at its center. She almost bit her lower lip when Adam lifted one of the candles, but managed to catch herself in time.

"I find the element of surprise is most effective for this particular punishment," Adam remarked conversationally, while Carly's heart kicked into overdrive. He set down the candle and picked up the sleep mask. Stroking Carly's hair away from her face, he slipped the mask over her eyes.

The first hot drop of wax landed on her stomach. Carly jerked, drawing in a sharp breath. A succession of hot droplets scattered over her torso, startling her each time, though she tried to ready herself. A scalding drop splashed over her left nipple and Carly gasped in pain. This was quickly followed by liquid wax falling over her right nipple and then trailing in a burning line between her breasts.

When the first drop landed on her spread cunt, Carly screamed. Her heart pounded and she felt the sweat beading on her forehead and upper lip. Her skin was on fire, and as the wax cooled against her flesh, another scalding droplet landed on a different spot. With each drop of melted wax Carly jerked in pain and surprise, causing the clamps to tug painfully at her labia.

"I can't," she began to gasp, barely aware she was speaking. "I can't, please, please, oh, oh, ow! I can't…"

"Of course you can, silly girl," she heard Adam say calmly over the rush of blood thundering in her ears. More wax scalded across her breasts and cunt, landing at the same time.

Tears were streaming from the corners of Carly's eyes, wetting the sleep mask. She couldn't stop panting, the breath rasping in her throat. She felt a hand on her cheek, its stroke gentle. "Slow down. Slow your breathing," Adam murmured. "Where is your discipline?"

Carly tried to obey, aware she was on the verge of hyperventilating. "Slow down," he repeated. "That's it. Deep breaths."

She felt something heavy placed on her abdomen and realized he'd balanced a candle there. "This will help you remember to slow your breathing. After all, you wouldn't want that to spill, would you?"

Carly shook her head, not trusting herself to speak. Every inch of exposed skin from chest to cunt was on fire beneath the drying crust of cooling wax. Her labia were numb from the compression, and her clit, despite the torture, was hard and throbbing.

She heard a thrumming and before she could identify the sound, the head of the vibrating wand covered her vulva, sending instant shockwaves of shivering pleasure through her loins.

"Fuck," she whispered, the word exploding from her lips before she could stop herself.

Adam chuckled softly, gently moving the vibrating ball over her spread vulva. Carly felt the shuddering rise of a climax, not the intense, all-consuming experience she'd had at Adam's touch, but more of a gut reaction, a manipulation of nerve endings resulting in a stimulus overload.

"Please, Sir," she managed to gasp, remembering the rules. "May I come?"

Adam said nothing. The wand continued to vibrate at her sex, the candle still balanced precariously on her shaking abdomen.

"Please," she begged again.

"No. Absolutely not. This is a punishment."

Yet still the wand buzzed at her clit. She tried in vain to twist her body away from the vibrator's constant stimulation, but only succeeded in nearly toppling the candle. Squeezing her eyes tight and clenching her teeth, she tried desperately to stave off the rising climax that threatened to take over her body.

She failed.

All at once the vibrator was removed, and the candle was lifted from her body. A second later a stream of searing wax splashed against her spread cunt and Carly screamed, jerking hard in her instinctive effort to slam her legs closed against the fiery onslaught of melted wax.

The clamps were released, sending an agonizing rush of blood to her labia, adding to the burning pain still washing over her vulva. Blindfolded and bound, not sure if he was done, not sure she could take another burning drop of wax or touch of the vibrator, Carly felt panic sliding over her like a shroud. She began to cry, jerking her head from side to side, her body taut and shaking.

She was dimly aware of Adam's removing the leather straps that held her down. He pulled the sleep mask from her eyes and then slid his arms beneath her, lifting her from the bondage chair and carrying her to the sofa.

Instead of settling there with her in his arms, as he'd done the night before, he plopped her down on her side and stepped back, staring down at her with a frown. "Calm down," he ordered, his tone terse. "You'd think you'd never been punished before. I did *not* give you permission to come. Have you no self control?" He glared at her.

"Go down to the master bathroom. You'll find wax removal lotion in the shower. Use it and then kneel in a corner in my bedroom until I come get you. I'm going to have lunch. I'll decide later if and when you can eat. I've a good mind to call the auction house and ask for someone who's better trained."

Carly watched in disbelieving horror through her tears as Adam turned on his heel and left the dungeon. Why hadn't she stopped him before it went too far? Why hadn't she used her safeword?

Because, she realized, she was afraid to use it. While Adam hadn't actually come out and said it, she understood that he expected more from her because of her supposed trained status as a professional sub girl. She'd lied on the auction application, claiming far more experience that she actually had in the scene. If Adam knew the sum total of her real training was all of a week, he'd probably send her packing that very day. She didn't dare admit just how untrained she in fact was—she couldn't risk it.

If he sent her back to the auction house, she wouldn't earn a dime of the bid price. She knew the trainers wouldn't let her participate in another auction if she was returned in such disgrace. She'd given up her room in the rent house and her job at the club for this chance. She was doing her very best. What the hell did he want from her?

"You bastard," Carly whispered vehemently at the absent Adam, fury overcoming fear. *You set me up. This is just some fucking game to you, but it's all I have right now.* Turning on her side, Carly curled into herself, trying to ignore the dry, annoying wax that covered the front of her body.

She lay there for several minutes alternating between feeling horribly sorry for herself and raging at Adam Wise for being such an impossible prick of a Master. Finally she pulled herself up and forced herself to go downstairs and shower. Whether this was a game or not, Adam was the one holding all the cards.

~*~

Adam bit into his roast beef sandwich as he stared unseeing at the newscast on the TV. He knew he'd been excessively harsh with Carly, but it had been her fault. She really seemed to have no orgasm control. While the man in him was gratified to think he could pull such powerful reactions from the girl, the Master in him was both surprised and annoyed at how poorly she seemed to be trained in this regard.

Still, had he pushed her too far? He had just assumed she could tolerate the combination of stimuli he'd thrown at her without really knowing her limits or capabilities.

Maybe this whole purchased slave thing was a bad idea from the start. Maybe he'd follow through on his threat and send her back. But who would he choose in her place? Would slave Nina be any different or any better? What the hell was he looking for anyway? A perfectly trained automaton who took every punishment with bland stoicism and orgasmed on command with the enthusiasm of a trained seal?

He took another bite of his sandwich and flicked off the TV. He knew what really troubled him, and he knew it was *his* fault.

He'd made her cry.

Not just the gasping cries of erotic suffering or pleasure, but actual tears, pulled from her because he hadn't properly gauged what she could or could not tolerate.

And what kind of Master didn't provide aftercare, especially after such an intense scene? Purchased or not, didn't she deserve at least that much? Yet instead of apologizing and soothing her, he'd let his anger at himself overflow onto her, and he'd blamed her for his own failure. He was no better than the bullies and posers he'd so despised at the BDSM clubs, the ones who used the guise of BDSM play to give vent to their hatred and fear of women.

Now the girl was probably kneeling in a corner, frightened he was going to send her back, worried she'd failed him, when in fact he was the one who had failed them both.

With a sigh, Adam started to push back from the table when his cell phone vibrated in his pocket. Pulling it out, he saw *James Sawyer* on the screen. James, though older by twenty years, was a good friend and a mentor when it came to BDSM.

James was something of a throwback, in Adam's estimation—one of those "one-woman" men, who had married his college sweetheart some forty years ago and had remained faithful to her ever since. Every other married man Adam knew thought nothing of carrying on one or even multiple affairs, or engaged in what Adam thought of as serial monogamy, working their way through new wives as casually as if they were buying a new car. Adam avoided the whole business, having learned long ago that love was for suckers and fools.

He considered letting the call go to voicemail, as he didn't really want to talk to anyone right now, but then he thought better of it. James was a thoughtful man, and not one to rush to judgment. If nothing else, maybe he'd have some advice on how Adam could salvage the situation.

"Hey, James," Adam said, connecting the call. "How are you?"

"I'm good, Adam. Doing fine. I thought I'd check in and see how it's going. Wasn't this the weekend you went to that slave auction?"

"Yep. I went last night. I came home with a beauty by the name of Carly."

"And how are things working out so far?" James had been less than enthusiastic when Adam had first told him of his idea to participate in the slave auction, mentioning in his mild, understated way that the arrangement seemed like one that could lead to a whole lot of trouble and complications. Adam had laughed that off at the time, assuring James he could handle whatever came his way. Now he wasn't so sure.

Adam cleared his throat. "Uh, okay. You know."

"I don't know." Adam could hear the smile in James' voice. "Why don't you tell me?"

Adam blew out a breath. "Well, things went well last night. She's very sexually responsive. I mean, she could be faking, but if so, she has me fooled." He laughed self-consciously, and then briefly described the auction process, the ride home and the events leading up to the wax play punishment.

"Sounds like you're not wasting a moment." James chuckled. "Amy is very curious to meet your slave girl." Amy was not only James' wife, but also his 24/7 slave. When not at work as a physician, she was kept naked and collared, and neither of them would have it any other way. Adam thought of Carly, upstairs and waiting, and his heart gave an uncomfortable lurch.

"The thing is," he began, faltering. "I mean, uh…"

"What is it, Adam? You sound troubled."

Adam rubbed his hand over his face. "I fucked up," he admitted in a rush. "I pushed her too far. I wasn't paying attention to her signals. Or I didn't read them correctly. I made her cry."

"Did she use her safeword?"

"No."

"Crying's not always a bad thing, Adam. Sometimes it's the place a sub needs to go. It's a kind of culmination, a release of everything that's going on, like a safety valve. Amy cries all the time after a really big orgasm. It's almost like laughing, except there are tears, though she insists she's not sad or hurt. It's just an overflow of emotion. It's not a negative thing. In fact, it can be very spiritually freeing, at least that's what Amy says."

Adam sighed. "These weren't tears of joy, trust me. And it gets worse. I was pissed off, really at myself more than her, though I wasn't seeing that at the time. The whole relationship is so artificial. I mean, if the word relationship can even be applied here. "I just"—he paused, thinking how he could clean this up, knowing there was no way, so he barreled on—"I just dumped her on the couch and left the dungeon. No aftercare, no nothing. I told her to get herself cleaned up and wait for me in a corner in my bedroom. She's up there now, at least I suppose she is, if she hasn't already packed her stuff."

James was silent for a moment, while Adam waited for his rebuke. James was very big into aftercare, and had counseled Adam on a number of occasions about its importance in establishing and maintaining an atmosphere of trust and safety necessary in a D/s relationship.

"This is new for you, Adam," James finally said. "I'm not sure I could do it, frankly—take that kind of responsibility for a woman I'd never met. It's sort of like an arranged marriage, if you think about it. But that doesn't mean you don't observe the basic conventions of such a union. Yes, you paid for her services, but from what I understand as you've described this whole thing, Carly has given herself to you in her promise to obey and submit to you, and that's very real, even if underlying it there's a cash transaction. She deserves the same respect and care as any submissive, don't you think?"

"Yeah," Adam said miserably. "I know."

"I sense you care for this girl. You want to make this work. You aren't ready to just cut your losses and start over, are you?"

"No. No way." Adam surprised himself with his sudden certainty, but couldn't deny it.

"Listen, Adam, just because you're the Dom, that doesn't mean you're perfect. And if this woman is worth her salt, she'll understand that. How old is she, anyway?"

"Thirty-two."

"Old enough to know what she's getting into, I would think, though at my age, you're all a bunch of spring chickens." James laughed. "Seriously, though, she's old enough to understand that people are human. They fuck up. They can be forgiven. Go to her now and explain the situation. Own up to where you let her down. Tell her how you'll stop that from happening in the future."

Adam stood, nodding. "Yes. Yes, I owe her that much. You're right. Thank you, James."

"Don't thank me. All I did was mirror back what you were saying. You already knew what to do."

They spoke a few minutes longer, and then Adam headed for the stairs, his new resolve urging him on. In the bedroom he saw Carly kneeling in the corner by his bureau, her face to the wall. Her wet hair fell in golden brown ringlets down her back. Her head was bowed, her forehead touching the wall.

"Carly," he said softly, stopping a few feet away from her. Abruptly she lifted her head, though she maintained her position with her face to the wall.

"Yes, Sir?"

Leaning down, he touched her shoulder. "Stand up. Turn around." She rose in a fluid, graceful movement and turned to face him, her eyes downcast. The skin on her breasts and torso was blotched pink and red, though whether it was burn marks or just a result of her scrubbing away the hardened wax, he couldn't say.

"Look at me." Adam put a finger beneath her chin, forcing her head up. She met his gaze. Her eyes and the tip of her nose were red, a tear still showing on one cheek. Impulsively Adam reached for it, flicking it gently away with his thumb.

"Come here," he said, leading her by the hand to the bed. "Sit beside me. I need to talk to you."

"Please," she blurted. "Don't send me back. I'll do anything. I'm sorry I messed up. It won't happen again, I swear. Please give me another chance."

"Carly, listen to me. I'm not sending you back. You didn't mess anything up. It was my fault. I came up to apologize."

"I'm sorry?" Carly looked blank, confusion in her eyes.

"For what happened up there. Yes, it was a punishment, and yes, you did come without permission, but I pushed you too far. I wasn't paying the right kind of attention to your reactions. I behaved in a way not suitable for a Dom. And then I left you alone, instead of offering you the aftercare you needed and deserved."

Adam realized he was still holding her hand. She was staring at him, her lips parted in surprise. "I let you down, Carly. I let us both down. It's me who needs to say it won't happen again."

"Oh," she said softly, and inexplicably her eyes filled again with tears.

"What, what is it? Don't cry. I'm the one to blame here. Not you. If you want to be returned to the auction house, I'll let them know in no uncertain terms that the fault was mine. I'm sure they'll let you stand for bidding again."

"No!" Carly burst out, pulling her hand from his and wrapping her arms protectively around her torso. Normally he would have called her on that, as it was unacceptable for a slave girl to hide her body at any time from her Master, but given the circumstances, he didn't comment.

Instead he echoed her. "No?"

"No," she said again, her voice pleading. "Don't send me back. Please, Sir. I have nowhere to go. Oh!" She clapped her hand over her mouth, as if the words she'd just uttered had escaped without her permission.

Nowhere to go?

This thought had never entered Adam's mind, not for a second. Surely she had *someplace* to go—a job from which she'd obtained a leave of absence, a home or an apartment, family she could return to.

"I mean," she added quickly, color washing over her cheeks, "I have this month set aside for this. I want to stay. I want to serve you, Sir. I want to please you."

And you want the money, Adam couldn't help thinking, but really, who could blame her for that? He nodded. "I appreciate that. Here's what I need from you if this is going to work. Don't be afraid to use your safeword. I might have given you the wrong impression earlier, but using the safeword isn't a sign of weakness. It just means I'm pushing you further than you're comfortable going, and if that's happening, you need to let me know. You might need your safeword because of the nature of our relationship, because I don't know you the way I would someone I had been involved with over a period of time. So it's essential that you communicate with me. If you really want to please me, that's the way to do it, okay?"

Carly nodded and then ducked her head, though not before he saw the wounded look in her eyes. What was that about? Deciding he would never understand women, he let it go. "Then it's settled.

Come down and have some lunch. Then we'll start over. Okay?"

"Yes, Sir. Thank you." Slipping from the bed, she knelt prettily in front of him and wrapped her arms around his legs, resting her cheek against his knee. "Thank you," she whispered again and Adam placed his hand on her hair, feeling the knot that had been tied around his heart for as long as he could remember loosen, if just a little.

Chapter 7

After lunch Adam, still contrite over the incident in the dungeon, told Carly she had an hour to do just exactly what she wanted to while he took care of a few things. She had opted for a soak in the Jacuzzi.

Adam returned to his study, intending to finish going through the financial reports of one of his subsidiaries that wasn't operating up to snuff. He found himself reading the same half page over and over. Giving up, he was just about to close the files when his cell phone rang. *James.* It was uncanny how the man knew when Adam needed him, even before Adam seemed to know it himself.

"Hey, James."

"Hey, Adam. Checking in to see how things are going with Carly. Everything good now?"

"Yeah, I think so, thanks," Adam replied. "I mean, I apologized and she seemed to accept it but..."

"But you want to do something more."

"Yeah. But I don't want to come across like some kind of wuss, either. I mean, I am supposed to be the Dom in this thing."

James laughed. "Okay, so you're the Dom. Doms do nice things for their subs. Why don't you take her out to dinner or something?"

All sorts of devious ideas instantly leaped into Adam's head. Then reality intervened. "She has nothing to wear. Not to the kind of place I'd like to take her."

"So? A mere detail. You run a multinational company, surely you can handle getting a woman an outfit." James laughed again, a big rumbling sound that always reminded Adam of a bear, if bears laughed. "What size is she?" James continued. "What's her coloring? Amy could help. She could select a few items from Saks for you and have them delivered to your house."

"Bergdorf Goodman," Adam said. "I have an account there."

Adam agreed to email James the details from Carly's slave dossier, along with her photos. James always had a knack for cutting to the chase and making the complicated seem suddenly easy.

With a plan in mind, Adam found himself able to concentrate. He was deeply engrossed in the financial reports when the doorbell rang. Lifting his head from the computer monitor, his first thought was of Carly, somewhere in the house, naked as a jaybird. But of course she would have the sense to stay out of sight. Glancing at his watch, he realized nearly three hours had passed since his call to James. He'd told Carly she had an hour. What in the world was she doing?

Leaving the study, Adam went to the front door. He tipped the young man holding out the clothing bags and hurried upstairs with them.

Adam found Carly asleep on the end of the bed, her shiny hair falling in a tumble of curls around her face. He draped the dress bags over the clothing rack and set the additional bags on the floor beside it. Walking toward the sleeping girl, he bent down and gently shook her shoulder.

"Carly. Wake up."

Carly sat bolt upright with a startled cry. "Oh! I'm sorry, Sir! I didn't realize I'd fallen asleep. I was waiting beside the bed but I wasn't sure when you were coming and then I guess I just lay down for a second and—"

"Shh, hush." Adam touched Carly's lips with two fingers. "It's okay."

He took away his fingers. Carly stared up at him, waiting. "We're going to go out to dinner tonight. *Le Carnard*. It's French and *très chic*." He smiled.

"Dinner?" Carly looked confused.

"That's what I said." He waved toward the clothing rack. "I had a few things ordered for you so you'll be suitably dressed. There are two dresses there in your size. Pick the one that suits you best. You'll also find shoes and stockings. The omission of bra and panties is intentional, so don't bother asking. You'll find your makup bag in the third drawer down on the left of your sink in the bathroom. You may use it, sparingly. I'll take care of the rest of your outfit. Come down to my study for inspection when you're dressed."

~*~

Adam entered the large walk-in closet, selecting various items of clothing for himself, which he took with him as he left her alone in the master bedroom. Carly sat on the edge of the bed staring at the opaque garment bags with BG stamped on them like a royal crest. She'd browsed at a few Berdorf Goodman year-end sales when she'd been gainfully employed, but even the sales had been too rich for her blood.

She found herself both pleased and excited at the prospect of his taking her out to a fine French restaurant. She was curious to see what he had picked out for her to wear. Inside the zipped bags she found a chiffon dress of royal blue. The other dress was a simple but elegant black sheath. She tried the dresses on in front of the full length three-way mirror, turning to see herself at all angles.

The blue dress was pretty, but seemed more like something one would wear to a wedding than to a night out. The black one fit as if it had been tailor-made for her, hugging her figure without being over-tight. It was evident by the poke of her nipples against the silky fabric that she wasn't wearing a bra, but that couldn't be helped.

Carly regarded herself in the mirror, touching the red slave collar at her throat. It was soft and narrow enough to pass for a choker, though the ring at its center might make someone wonder. Since Adam hadn't said anything about taking it off, she would leave it in place.

There were two pairs of shoes as well, and she selected the black sandals with tiny seed pearls embroidered along the sides. The heels were higher than she would normally wear, but this wasn't about her comfort she reminded herself.

There was also a black satin garter belt and two packages of stockings, one nude, the other a sheer black. Carly chose the black stockings. They had a shimmery, silky sheen that made her feel very elegant as she slid them over her legs.

When she presented herself in Adam's study, he was busy typing something on his keyboard. She stood quietly for a few moments just inside the door, not sure what to do or if he even knew she was there.

Finally she dared to interrupt. "I'm ready, Sir. For the inspection."

Adam typed for a few more seconds and then swiveled toward her. "I was just finishing..." His words trailed off as he looked at her. "My, my. Very nice." Carly smiled uncertainly, relieved he seemed pleased. She had swept her unruly curls back in a French twist and sprayed them into submission, letting ringlets strategically escape at her neck and temples. Remembering Adam's directive to use her makeup sparingly, she had used a sheer foundation to smooth away any imperfections, a little blush and mascara, and just a hint of shimmering pale gold eye shadow.

Standing, Adam picked up a small cloth bag from his desk and approached her. He was dressed in dark, well-fitting trousers and a showy white button-down shirt with gold cufflinks and an elegant silk tie.

Opening the bag, he removed its contents, setting the items on the edge of the desk along with a tube of lubricant. Carly saw a slim black butt plug in cellophane wrapping, four silver balls the size of large marbles on a string and a small rubber butterfly vibrator with elastic bands attached to it.

"You know what all these items are, I presume?" Carly nodded, nearly biting her lip, biting the inside of her cheek instead. Adam held up the butt plug, pulling off the wrapper. "This is quite flexible so you shouldn't have any problem accommodating it while sitting."

Taking the tube of lubricant along with the plug, Adam pulled a large leather ottoman away from the chair against which it was placed. "Lift your dress to your waist and lie down over this ottoman on your stomach. Spread your ass cheeks for me and be still."

Carly knelt carefully over the ottoman, mindful of her stockings against the carpet. Reaching back, she spread her cheeks, trying not to clench her muscles in anticipation of the invading phallus. It went in easily, with only the last bit where it flared causing any discomfort.

"Turn over and spread your legs, your back on the ottoman, feet flat on the floor. Keep your dress up around your waist." While Carly obeyed, Adam stood and pointed toward the ben wa balls and the butterfly vibrator. "These are a custom-made set. Both the butterfly and the balls have tiny batteries inside, activated by this." Reaching in the pocket of his trousers, he pulled out what looked like a very small TV remote control with a daisy wheel embedded on one side. When he pressed the on button, the balls vibrated and bounced against the desktop, and the butterfly vibrator hummed quietly beside them.

Flicking off the remote, Adam reached for the toys. He crouched on the carpet between Carly's knees. Pushing her legs wider, he stroked her cunt with lubricated fingers until she had to press her lips together to keep from moaning. With a knowing smile, he squirted more of the lubricant onto the silver balls and then inserted them, one by one, inside of her.

Rising again, Adam held up the rubber butterfly. "This will serve as your underwear tonight. Stand up and pull it on, just like you would a pair of panties."

Standing carefully because of the butt plug, Carly took the offered vibrator and slipped her legs into the elastic ties, drawing them up to rest on her hips. Her dress remained hiked up around her waist. Reaching between her legs, Adam adjusted the position of the butterfly so it fit snugly between her labia, the underside nestled squarely against her clit. The elastic straps around her hips held the vibrator in place.

This time when Adam pressed the remote, both the balls and the butterfly vibrated against and inside her, sending instant waves of stimulating pleasure through her body. Adam slid his finger over the wheel on the side of the remote, causing the vibrations to quicken and intensify.

"Oooo," Carly gasped, at once startled and aroused by the sensations, which were heightened by the phallus filling her ass.

"Yes, *oh*." Adam's grin was evil. He flicked the remote off and placed it back into his pocket. "You can put your dress down."

Striding toward the door of the study, Adam reached behind it and removed his jacket from its hanger, draping it over one shoulder. Looking back at her, he said, "You have one job this evening, Carly. That is to behave with proper decorum while we're out." As he spoke, his hand slid into his pocket. The sudden vibrating hum and jiggle of the balls and butterfly at her sex made Carly gasp in startled surprise.

It was, she realized with chagrin, going to be a long night.

~*~

"We'll both have *le diner prix fixe*," Adam told the waiter, waving away the offered ala carte menus.

"*Très bien, Monsieur.*" The elderly waiter offered a small, formal bow and retreated.

The sommelier appeared with a bottle of white wine. Once he'd opened it, had Adam give his approval and then filled their glasses, he set the wine into an iced bucket and faded away.

Adam reached for his glass and sipped. Carly did the same. "The food here is amazing," he said. "I trust you don't mind that I took the liberty of ordering for us both." As he spoke, Adam slipped his free hand into his pocket and flicked the wheel of the remote to its lowest setting.

Carly's eyes widened, her lips pressing together as she took in what he'd done. Adam regarded her in amused silence as she shifted in her chair, crossing and uncrossing her legs, clearly trying to maintain her composure.

The waiter returned with their first course, mackerel in a delicate wine sauce. Carly nodded to the waiter when he held the huge pepper grinder in her direction. Adam chose that moment to up the intensity on the remote, pulling a startled, breathless gasp from his companion.

Abruptly the waiter pulled back. "My apologies, Madame. Too much pepper?"

"No, no, it's fine," Carly managed, casting an anguished look in Adam's direction. He only smiled and reached for his fork.

When the waiter had once again discreetly melted into the background, Adam rolled the wheel back to low, just a vibrating whir to remind Carly of his control. Other than breathing a little more rapidly than normal, she managed to eat her fish with reasonable calm.

Two waiters arrived with the braised lamb and vegetables, along with the sommelier bearing a bottle of red wine. As they hovered solicitously over the table, Adam turned up the intensity of Carly's toys once again, watching as his slave girl struggled to keep her composure.

All three men serving them kept casting surreptitious glances Carly's way, no doubt admiring the flush on her creamy skin, the perk of those gorgeous nipples beneath her dress and the delightful way she was squirming in her seat. The youngest waiter stayed after the sommelier and the older Frenchman had gone, lingering unnecessarily, it seemed to Adam.

"You may go," Adam informed him. "We'll let you know if we need anything else."

Carly had her hands on the table now, pressing down with open palms. Her eyes were closed, her face twisted in concentration. When the waiter had gone, she whispered urgently, "Please, Sir. Please. I'm going to come. I can't help it. Please."

"If you do, I'll punish you. And I won't wait till we get home either. You'll be punished right here in the restaurant."

Her eyes flew open, her hands clenching into fists. Adam glanced around them. They were seated in a private corner of the restaurant and the lighting was dim. As long as no waiter suddenly appeared, no one would witness what was happening at their table.

Carly was visibly sweating now, a sheen on her flushed cheeks. Her hands were clenched in her lap and her body was shaking. "Oh, god. I can't help it. Oh god…" A sweet whimper escaped her lips and she lifted a hand to her mouth, trying to stifle her small orgasmic cries.

"Did you come?" Adam asked unnecessarily as he flicked off the remote.

Sagging back against her chair, Carly nodded. "I'm sorry, Sir. I couldn't help—"

"Yes, yes, I know," Adam interrupted, pretending to be annoyed. "You couldn't help it. First thing tomorrow we'll work on orgasm control, young lady. But for now, enjoy your food before it gets cold. Punishment comes afterwards."

That was mean, he knew, and Adam felt almost bad for having possibly ruined her ability to enjoy her meal, but, after a few hesitant bites, Carly began to eat, the incredible food no doubt overshadowing any anxiety about the impending punishment at least for the moment.

As they shared their meal, Carly kept casting the occasional anxious look Adam's way. Adam smiled benignly back at her. The younger waiter appeared every few minutes, refilling a water glass, offering fresh bread, topping off their wine, his eyes sliding hungrily over Carly when he thought no one was looking.

When the main course was cleared, the older Frenchman appeared, a crisp white linen napkin over his arm, the younger waiter in tow just behind him. "Are you ready for your coffee and dessert, Monsieur?"

"In a bit," Adam replied, pushing back his chair. "We're going to take some air. We'll be back in about ten minutes."

"*Très bien, Monsieur.*" The man bowed while the younger waiter pulled Carly's chair back for her. The waiters probably assumed they were going out for a smoke, but Adam led Carly back to the restrooms.

There were five separate restrooms, each with its own private door. Inside was more like a small living room than a bathroom. There was a walled-off stall for the toilet. Along with a marbled sink, the small room contained a long, low sofa with a thickly-piled throw rug in front of it.

Adam sat on the sofa and reached into the inner pocket of his jacket for the travel quirt he had placed there in anticipation of this delicious moment. "Lift your dress to your waist," he ordered the still-standing girl, "and lie on your stomach over my lap."

Carly drew in her breath as she stared at the wicked leather whip in his hand, but did as he ordered. Adam could feel his cock rising beneath her body resting so sweetly on his, but now wasn't the time for his pleasure.

"Five strokes on each side. You will count."

The base of the butt plug was peeking from between her cheeks and he could just see the edges of the rubber butterfly pressed against her pussy. He thought about turning the toys on again, but decided that would distract from Carly's focus on the quirt.

Pressing one hand firmly against the small of her back to keep her steady, Adam brought the dual strips of stiff leather down hard against her ass. "One!" Carly gasped, as two small welts rose side by side on her skin, perpendicular to the satin garters.

"Two! Oh!" she cried as the whip again met its target.

"Keep your voice down," Adam said, as he struck her again. "You don't want them to hear you out there, do you?"

When he was done, Adam pushed Carly gently from his lap, letting her roll to her knees on the rug. "Look at me," he commanded.

Carly lifted her face to him. Her eyes were bright with tears, her cheeks flushed, several escaped ringlets of hair framing her face. Adam wanted nothing more at that moment than to push her down to the ground and fuck her silly.

Instead he stood, replacing the quirt in its inner pocket. He reached into an outer pocket and handed Carly the small pocketbook he'd allowed her to pack with lipstick and other feminine essentials. "Make yourself presentable and come back to the table. I'll be waiting for you."

Once seated again, Adam nodded toward the hovering waiters. In a few minutes Carly returned to the table, fresh lipstick on her pretty mouth, her hair once again more or less in place. Adam hid his smile as he watched her lower herself gingerly to the chair, her bottom no doubt smarting from the whipping.

Fresh raspberries with apricot honey cream were set before them along with china cups of steaming coffee and snifters of fine Cognac. As Carly speared a raspberry, Adam turned on the remote, causing her dessert fork to tinkle against the crystal bowl.

Carly looked at him with a beseeching gaze, but he stared her down, silently daring her to protest. She took a deep breath and looked down. "Eat," Adam admonished with a grin. "And try that brandy. It's quite excellent."

Carly managed to eat several raspberries and even added cream and sugar to her coffee, though her hand trembled. She sipped at the brandy and Adam pushed the remote wheel higher, causing her to set her snifter down with a clunk as she gasped.

Adam watched the play of emotion move over her flushed features—she wanted to protest, he could see that, but she, wisely, didn't dare. A shudder moved through her body as she clutched and twisted the linen napkin in her lap.

Adam sipped the strong coffee as he enjoyed her show, glad the jacket would hide the raging erection pulsing between his legs when they left the restaurant. "Come for me," he finally said in a soft voice, rolling the wheel to high.

Carly's shudders had barely subsided when the young waiter approached, a silver coffee pot in his hand. "More coffee, Monsieur? Madame?" Though he addressed them both, the young man had eyes only for Carly, who had wrapped her arms around her torso, her chest still heaving from her recent orgasm.

"No, thanks," Adam said, holding out a credit card. "I think we're all done here."

Chapter 8

The room flickered in the candlelight, revealing vaulted ceilings and walls draped in flowing gold silk. The slave was dressed in swirling, sheer scarves that revealed as much as they hid, gold and silver chains at her wrists and ankles. She danced around him, her hair flying. He tried to see her face, but it was hidden beneath a veil. Several more women were kneeling around him as he lay back against the silk cushions.

Adam lifted the goblet of hot, spiced wine to his lips, but forgot to drink as one of the slave girls lowered her head over his lap, closing soft lips over his erect shaft. Adam could feel his cock hardening to steel. He reached for the girl's hair, which fell in long, silky ringlets. Gripping tightly, he pulled her head down, forcing her to take the full length of him.

As cool fingers curled around his balls, Adam slowly opened his eyes. He was still caught in the web of his dream, though the woman at his groin was no dream. Lifting his head, Adam saw Carly's tousled mop of curls bouncing against his stomach. His head fell back against the pillows and he closed his eyes again, letting the dream swirl back around him with the scents of cardamom and melting beeswax.

Carly lowered her head, taking the full length of him. She was doing something amazing with her throat muscles against the head of his cock. Again Adam reached for handfuls of her hair, gripping the silky tresses and wrapping them around his knuckles.

He held her in that position, aware she probably couldn't breathe with his cock so far down her throat. The dream burned away in the face of Adam's lust. How long could she hold her breath before she began to struggle and push against him? How obedient was she? Would she let him hold her there until she passed out?

When he let her go, she reared back, sucking in a gasping breath, but then she plunged back down, suckling and stroking his shaft with increased fervor, her silky tresses flying over his skin. Adam felt the rise of an orgasm, his balls tightening with expectation. He realized he didn't want to come yet.

"Slow down," he murmured. "Make it last." He pushed gently at her head, and Carly obeyed, releasing her suckling grip. She began to kiss his cock with closed lips, light, feathery kisses that almost tickled as she moved from head to base and back again.

She was crouched between his spread thighs on the mattress, and now she scooted back, changing her focus to Adam's balls, which she took one at a time into her mouth, gently licking the sensitive skin. As she moved, Adam felt a hard nipple brush his thigh. His cock twitched as he imagined sucking each nipple in turn to a shiny pink pebble. He started to reach down to pull her up to him so he could do just that, but stopped himself in time. Carly was not his lover, but his paid slave girl, and she was doing the morning task she had been assigned, nothing more.

Letting his eyes close, Adam contented himself with the pleasure of her tongue and soft fingers moving over his cock and balls. He felt her shifting between his legs and she put her hands on his thighs, gently pushing them farther apart. Moving her head lower against him, Adam felt her tongue gliding along his perineum as she pushed up against his thighs with surprising strength.

The touch of her hot, wet tongue against his asshole sent a jolt of confused pleasure rippling through Adam's loins. Carly rimmed his asshole for several seconds, her hands finding and gripping his shaft and balls as she licked. He hadn't asked for that. He wasn't even sure what he thought about it.

He stopped thinking when the tip of her tongue pressed its way past the ring of muscle while her hands continued to milk his cock until he moaned, a low feral sound pulled from somewhere deep inside him.

Carly was moaning too—soft breathy sounds as she licked and stroked him, her hips undulating against the mattress as if she were riding an invisible cock. Forgetting his resolve, Adam reached for the girl, pulling her body upward and twisting her so he could get at the sweetmeat between her legs.

She groaned as he lapped at her silky folds. His nostrils filled with the delicate sweetness of her musk and he gripped her hips to hold her there. Carly was twisting against him, her hot, wet mouth finding his cock. Her lips moved with perfect suction over his throbbing shaft as he buried his face between her legs. He flicked his tongue against the hard nubbin at her center, teasing around it in looping circles until she squealed against his shaft, tremors moving through her body.

"Oh, oh, oh," she began to cry. And then, "Please, Sir, oh! May I come, oooo..." She closed her lips again around his cock, her body shaking.

Adam stopped his kisses long enough to respond. "Yes. Come for me, slave girl." She shuddered against him, though her mouth remained sheathed around his shaft. He could feel the pulse at her clit, which was hard as a small marble against his tongue.

Adam felt a slim finger slipping into his ass just as the tide of a blinding orgasm crashed through him, causing him to spurt into the silky warmth of Carly's mouth. He could feel Carly swallowing against him, but she kept the shaft in her mouth as they lay there, legs akimbo, hearts pounding.

When Adam's cock began to soften, Carly let it slip from her mouth and lowered her head to lick his balls, her tongue moving in a figure eight from one to the other until Adam finally reached down and pulled her into his arms.

Carly nuzzled her head against the hollow between his neck and shoulder. Adam lay in a kind of sexual stupor, stroking her hair, loving the feel of it gliding through his fingers, savoring the press of her warm body against his.

And then the light flicked back on in his head.

Holy shit.

What the hell did he think he was doing?

Sitting abruptly, he pushed the girl from him and swung his legs over the side of the bed. What the hell had just happened? He'd been half asleep, those fevered, silken dreams dictating his behavior. He stared down at Carly, at the sated, sleepy smile on her lips and the way her hair flung out in all directions, a tangle of golden-brown curls spreading over the pillow. He drank in her full, lush breasts, the tips still rosy hard.

He felt a rush of confused anger pushing through him, but had learned enough from the day before to recognize the blame lay with himself. He wouldn't make that mistake a second time. But that didn't change the fact that he was getting in too deep with this whole thing.

He needed to pull back and focus on why he'd bought this girl in the first place.

Erotic BDSM play, no strings attached, end of story.

It was up to him to reassert his control of both the situation and the naked girl lying like a lover in his bed. "Get up and shower," he said, striving to keep the brusqueness from his tone. This wasn't her fault. He had allowed it. It was up to him to fix it. "I'll be back to inspect and mark you in fifteen minutes."

Without waiting for her to react or respond, Adam turned on his heel and left the room, heading for the guest bedroom. A hot shower and a strong cup of coffee would clear his head. And after that, he'd introduce Carly to the water chamber.

~*~

Carly showered in a daze, her mind fogged from the endorphins still rippling through her body. As the hot water cascaded over her, her mind began to switch back on, shining a light on the jumble of confused thoughts whirling through her head.

She still wasn't sure what the heck had happened. She had started out with the sole intention of making Adam come per his morning instructions, but something had taken over her body, completely bypassing her brain. She'd found herself licking, suckling, *worshipping* Adam's body with the devotion of a lover. With each stroke of her tongue and caress of her fingers she had felt herself sliding deeper into a submissive headspace she'd rarely experienced in her life, the kind of headspace she'd thought was reserved for someone in love.

In love...

Vigorously Carly rubbed the shampoo into her scalp, as if she could scrub the very idea away. There was no way she was *in love* with this guy! First of all, she'd only been with him a few days. Second of all, she was nothing more than a commodity to him — a plaything with an already predetermined expiration date. Who could love someone like that, someone who chose to *buy* what should be given freely?

She shook her head beneath the water and mouthed the word *no*. If and when she ever fell in love again, it would be with someone who valued her not only as a submissive sex object, but as a woman, as a person.

And yet...

The way he'd pulled her to him, flipping her body, his mouth closing over her sex, his tongue and fingers moving in such a way that she was trembling within seconds — his had been a lover's touch, hadn't it? Or was it really just an extension of his control — he did it because he could, because he understood how to touch a woman, how to draw reactions. That didn't necessarily mean anything beyond the fact that he was sexually skilled and attuned to a woman's body. She'd already learned that the first night in the car. It was nothing new, so why did things feel so different this morning?

After rinsing and conditioning her hair, Carly began to groom her body, carefully smoothing away any stubble with her razor. She worked quickly and efficiently. Rinsing the conditioner from her hair, she stepped out of the shower and dried herself.

Carly stood waiting in the bedroom, her fingers laced behind her neck, her legs shoulder-width apart. She took a deep breath and blew it out slowly, silently promising herself to keep her emotions in check going forward, no matter what curves Adam threw her way. She needed to keep her emotional distance if she was to survive this month as his toy.

He came into the bedroom in just a pair of cargo shorts, his damp hair curling down his neck, his eyes sweeping her body. He was holding a small leather quirt in one hand, a large glass of water in the other. As he approached her, she could smell his freshly soaped skin and couldn't help but admire his muscular pecs and biceps.

"Drink this," he instructed, holding the glass out to her. "All of it."

Though Carly would have preferred her morning coffee, she was rather thirsty and, without thinking too much about it, she drank down the fresh, cool water. Adam took the empty glass from her and set it down on the bureau.

"Resume your position," he said, returning to her. "Hands behind your head, legs spread wide." Once she had reassumed the inspection position, Adam stroked his fingers over her body. When he got to her cunt, he slid a finger between her labia, the tip brushing her hooded clit and moving back to press inside of her. Carly couldn't stop the tremor that moved through her body at his touch. At the same time he reached for her throat with his other hand as his clear gray eyes looked past her face and into her secrets.

For a moment Carly thought he was going to say something about what had happened between them in the bed that morning, but he said nothing as he stared into her eyes. The feel of his fingers on her throat softened something inside her, as such a touch always did. She realized she wanted to wrap her arms around his body and pull his face down to hers. So much for keeping her distance.

A small smile quirked along one side of Adam's mouth and Carly had the disquieting feeling he had just read her thoughts. She felt herself coloring and she wanted to look away, but Adam's strong fingers on her throat held her fast.

Just think of the money, she tried to tell herself. *That's all that matters.*

But she knew she was lying. God help her, she was falling for this guy, and there didn't seem to be a thing she could do to stop it.

Finally releasing her, Adam pointed to the low stool and Carly draped herself over it, her ass tingling in anticipation of the quirt's stroke. It came fast, a searing sting over both cheeks.

Gripping a handful of her wet hair, Adam pulled Carly to her feet. "It's early. Before we have breakfast, I'm going to take you down to the water chamber. I assume you're familiar with erotic water play?"

Carly's mind flashed to the site she'd sometimes perused online — a water bondage site where girls were bound in rope and dunked into pools, or chained against a wall and sprayed with powerful hoses. Her stomach clenched in nervous anticipation at the thought Adam might want to do that to her. While she had no fear of water, the thought of that kind of play frightened her. She gave voice to none of her musings, not wanting to come across as the novice she in fact was.

"Yes, Sir," she replied.

"Good."

Reaching into one of the many pockets in his shorts, Adam withdrew a slim metal leash, which he attached to her collar. Using the leash, he led Carly out of the bedroom and down the stairs. Adam took her through the large dining room, past a table that seated twelve. Between the dining room and the kitchen was an old-fashioned butler's pantry with a door at the far end that opened on a set of descending stairs.

The basement at the bottom of the stairs had white walls, the floor covered in black and white checked linoleum. There was a fancy washer and dryer set against one wall, with a stainless steel sink and folding counter beside them. Shelves lined the back wall filled with various tools, cans of paint and the usual paraphernalia that accumulated in household basements.

Adam led Carly through the room to a locked door on the far wall. Taking a set of keys from one of his pockets, he unlocked the door and pushed it open. Once inside, Adam removed Carly's leash and flicked on the light.

The walls and ceiling of this second spacious room were tiled like an indoor pool, the floor covered with thick rubber matting, drains set at intervals throughout the room. What looked like a huge fish tank occupied most of one wall, the water inside tinted pale blue by lights set beneath it. The tank was covered with a folding lid, like the kind used on outdoor hot tubs. It was flanked on either side by thick, sturdy-looking platforms. Hanging from a winch in the ceiling above it were half a dozen thick chains with large clips attached to their ends.

Tearing her gaze from the tub, Carly saw there were several black hoses neatly coiled and hanging on hooks along one wall, with faucets near the ground beneath them. On a perpendicular wall there were thick eyebolts embedded into the concrete at various intervals with plastic cuffs dangling from them by chains.

The room was warm but that didn't stop the shiver of apprehension that moved through Carly's naked body as she wrapped her arms protectively around her torso. There had been no water play training during the weeklong intensive at the auction house. She stared with naked fear at the water tank and thought about what she hadn't revealed in her dossier. What if she couldn't handle whatever it was Adam had planned for her?

Adam moved toward the tub and lifted back the lid. Steam rose from the water. He turned toward Carly, his eyes glittering. "Imagine yourself with your arms bound tightly at your sides, your body crisscrossed in a webbing of thick rope. You would be suspended from those chains and then lowered, inch by inch, until you were under the water, your very breath controlled by another, your life, quite literally, in his hands."

Auction, Carly reminded herself. *That's my safeword. I can use it if I need it.* Wait! How would she use her safeword if she was submerged in the water? She opened her mouth, about to ask for permission to speak, but closed it as Adam continued.

"It takes extraordinary trust between two people to engage in the kind of intense breath play this submersion tank makes possible. While I know your contract says nothing regarding hard limits when it comes to water play, I don't believe you're ready yet for that kind of scenario."

Carly felt relief pulse through her body and she blew out the breath she hadn't realized she'd been holding. "No, Sir," she whispered gratefully.

Her relief was short-lived, however, as Adam said, "This morning we'll see how you handle the spray. But before we do that, you're going to pee for me."

"I'm sorry, what, Sir?" She had heard him, but hoped she had not heard him correctly.

"You're going to squat over that drain" — Adam pointed to the drain set into the concrete near the hoses — "and empty your bladder. I'm going to watch. After that, I'll hose you down."

Carly flashed back to Patty at the auction house. Her refusal to pee in front of the others had resulted in her dismissal from the program. At the time Carly had been deeply, silently grateful that she hadn't been the one called upon to squat on the newspaper like a puppy. Now she understood all too well why Adam had her drink that large glass of water.

Carly took a deep breath. She could do this. What was the big deal? She blew out the air slowly, willing herself to be calm and graceful. Graceful! That was a laugh. She felt awkward and humiliated as she forced herself to squat over the drain.

At least her bladder was full. She closed her eyes to Adam's intense scrutiny and thought of flowing water.

Nothing happened.

"Go on. Are you disobeying me?" Adam demanded.

Carly opened her eyes. "No, Sir! At least, not on purpose. I'm trying. It's—it's kind of embarrassing, Sir."

Master Franklin's words moved through her mind. *Modesty,* he had said, *implies boundaries. It implies your separateness from your Master. A true slave gives up her modesty as a gift to her Master.*

Carly felt the sudden easing of her muscles and the warm stream of urine splashing down between her legs. She closed her eyes again, aware she was blushing, but relieved she'd been able to obey Adam.

"Good girl," Adam said warmly. Mixed with her embarrassment, Carly experienced an odd sense of pride. She had done what he'd asked of her, despite her reservations. She had worked past her modesty. She had pleased her Master.

Adam pulled Carly up by the arm and positioned her with her back against the concrete wall between the eyebolts. Reaching for her wrists, he lifted them, pressing them against the wall over her head. "Stay in that position. I'm going to chain you in place."

Grasping the chains on either side of her, Adam pulled the cuffs open and secured her wrists against the wall. He did the same thing with her ankles, so she was spread eagle against the cool concrete. "Arch your pelvis, show me that cunt," Adam ordered, tapping her hip. Carly tried to obey, though it was difficult to move, chained as she was.

Adam moved toward the wall with the hoses and reached for one, uncoiling it from its spool. Bending down, he turned on a faucet and held his fingers beneath the running water for several seconds before turning it off to attach the hose.

Carly's heart was beating high in her throat. She tried to take several deep, calming breaths, but each one came out in a shuddery gasp. Adam came to stand in front of her. He reached for the hair that had fallen into her eyes, pushing it from her face. His touch was gentle, his expression kind, though his eyes seemed to be glittering with an inner fire that made Carly catch her breath.

For one ridiculous second she thought he was going to kiss her, but he only leaned down to whisper in her ear. "Calm yourself, Carly. Slow your breathing. Show me your grace." He stroked her cheek, his fingers sliding sensually down her throat. "I won't give you more than you can handle." His hands found her nipples, catching them between thumbs and forefingers, rolling them like marbles as they stiffened to his touch.

When they were fully erect, he twisted hard, all the while looking deep into her eyes. Carly winced as the pain shot through her nipples, but then moaned as it went zipping along her nerve endings to lodge directly in her cunt, which she could feel swelling and moistening between her spread legs. Adam offered a knowing smile as he let her go and stepped back.

He moved toward the hose and returned to stand in front of her. Pointing the nozzle at her groin, he squeezed the lever, sending a spray of water in her direction. Reflexively Carly closed her eyes, expecting a freezing blast, but the water that hit her skin was surprisingly, even pleasantly, warm. He sprayed her sex and rinsed away the dribble of pee that had slid down her thigh.

Adam moved the spray over her body, drawing it under her arms and along her sides, playing it over her breasts, aiming it at her nipples. "You have one job this morning. That is *not* to come. You *will* exhibit self control. No orgasm. Not unless or until I say so. Is that understood?"

"Yes, Sir," Carly gasped, again squeezing her eyes shut as the spray splashed into her face.

Adam turned the head of the nozzle and the spray became a more focused stream of water that he aimed between her legs. "Give me that cunt," he ordered in a hoarse voice. Carly saw the erection tenting beneath his shorts. "Arch it forward," he commanded, and she struggled in her chains to obey.

The jet stream hit her spread pussy in an explosion of warm, pounding water, instantly sending jolts of sensation through her body—not precisely pleasure, not precisely pain, but definitely intense. Just when the pressure was nearly too much to bear, he shifted the spray, moving it over her body in no particular pattern.

Then it was back at her cunt, vibrating the delicate folds and pounding against her clit in a steady stream. "Oh god," she heard herself groan. *Don't come, don't come. Think of something else. Tax returns. A root canal. Don't come. Don't come.*

She tried to twist her body away, but Adam barked, "Cunt out. Don't you dare shift away."

The spray pelted her sex, a steady, sharp stream of relentless stimulation. As the water continued to pound at her clit, Carly's body began to judder of its own accord, an orgasm building against the flimsy dam of her self control, despite her desperate attempts to resist. *Car trouble, getting fired, no place to live...*

It didn't work. She couldn't fight the rising surge of climactic release being forced from her body by the masturbatory fingers of the water stream. Giving in, she felt her head fall back against the wall, her wrists and ankles straining against their cuffs, her heart bursting in her chest as the orgasm was wrested from her unwilling body.

For a moment she couldn't figure out where she was, and why she was dripping wet. Then it came rushing back, and she realized she must have blacked out for a second or two. Adam had dropped the hose and was standing in front of her, shaking his head with a bemused expression.

He reached for her wrists cuffs, pulling them free. Crouching, he released her ankles as well. As she stepped away from the wall on rubbery legs, Adam moved toward a cabinet near the door that Carly hadn't noticed before. He took out a thick, white terrycloth robe, which he draped around Carly's shivering shoulders.

To her surprise, he took her into his arms, cradling her against his body. Tentatively, she dared to wrap her own arms around his waist, ready to instantly retreat if he gave any sign that she was overstepping. But he only held her tighter, and she could feel his cheek against the side of her head, and his hard, muscular chest against her breasts. What she really wanted, she realized as he held her, was a kiss.

What she got instead was a pat on the bottom, and then he dropped his arms and stepped back to look at her. "What am I going to do with you, Carly? You can't obey the simplest command." His eyes were twinkling, but the curve of his mouth was cruel, and Carly knew she was going to be punished for her lack of self control.

"I think I know what we'll work on after breakfast and chores today," he said, using a towel to dry his own wet torso. "Any slave girl worth her salt needs to learn to control her orgasm." Pulling her leash from his pocket, Adam attached it to the wet leather collar around her neck. Giving it a light tug, he added nonchalantly, "We'll begin right after your whipping."

Chapter 9

Carly's arms were extended over her head, her wrists cuffed to chains hanging from a beam in the dungeon's ceiling. She was stretched taut, her legs spread wide and held in place by cuffs hooked to bolts in the floor by each ankle.

Adam walked around her in a slow, continuous circle, striking her body with the heavy flogger, its leather tresses stinging her skin as they snapped against her ass, her thighs, her breasts, her shoulders. She could feel the sweat pricking beneath her underarms, and the rush of breath rising in her throat. When he flicked the leather between her spread legs Carly jerked hard and gave a startled cry of pain. When the tips of the leather caught at her nipples, she gasped and began to pant.

Adam continued to move in a circle around her as he flogged her, his movements almost lazy as he let the stinging leather land against her body. When he began to speak, Carly had to concentrate to make sense of his words over the ragged pant of her own breath and the sparks of fiery pain showering her skin.

"Erotic suffering can come in many forms," he was saying. "This pain you feel now as the leather kisses your skin"—he struck her breasts with a stinging thwack—"is easily identifiable by your brain as pain. But there are different ways to suffer, ways we will explore together." He struck her ass, the tips of the leather tresses curling cruelly around her hip.

The flogger swished and whirled around her body, covering every inch of her flesh until Carly felt as if her skin were being flayed from her body, her breath pushed from her lungs in hiccupping cries. She was dizzy and might have fallen if she hadn't been held up by chains, her feet locked into place. As it was, she sagged heavily against the wrist cuffs, her chin dropping onto her chest.

When he finally let her down, Carly fell to her knees, a wave of dizziness moving over her, her mind a fog. Adam crouched beside her, stroking the hair from her face. His touch was gentle as he helped her to a more comfortable sitting position on the carpet. He sat beside her. She could smell his clean soap scent and the hint of masculine sweat. She could feel the heat of his skin near hers. To keep herself from reaching for him, she drew up her legs, wrapping her arms around her knees.

Adam pushed himself to his feet and smiled down at her. "That was your punishment. Now comes your training."

He walked toward the bookshelf. Carly watched with open-mouthed surprise as he pressed a button on the wall, causing the entire shelf to slide into some kind of hidden panel, like something out of a Victorian horror novel.

Behind the shelf was a small chamber, most of the space filled by a black leather bondage table complete with belts, cuffs, hooks and chains set strategically along the edges to fully immobilize a person in any number of positions. There were stirrups attached to the corners on either side at the end of the table.

Adam turned to Carly with an evil grin, the corners of his eyes crinkling into laugh lines. "You never know what you'll find in some of these old houses." He moved toward her, extending a hand. "Come on. I'm going to strap you down and we'll have a nice, long lesson in orgasm control. We'll practice every day, as long as it takes. You *will* learn to control your body and your reactions, or you'll continue to pay the price."

Carly allowed him to pull her upright and she moved toward the small chamber with trepidation. There was a long, high counter set against the back wall, on top of which were rows of neatly placed whips, handcuffs, ball gags, coils of rope, lengths of chain and half a dozen dildos and vibrators, each wrapped in shrink plastic. What really got Carly's attention, however, was what looked like a small red plastic gun with a narrow twelve-inch rod coming from the muzzle, its tip ending in a rubber-tipped fork that reminded Carly of a scorpion's tail.

Adam followed her gaze, his lips lifting in a cruel smile. "I can see by your expression you're familiar with this." He lifted the shock prod, his finger curling around the trigger. When he pressed it, sparks flew from the forked tip, making Carly jump. "Got your attention, huh? Nothing like a zap from this baby to remind you to obey. I'll only use it if you make me. It's all up to you, Carly."

He directed her toward the bondage table, helping her to lie down. He had her scoot to the end of the table and place her feet into the stirrups. He used Velcro straps over her ankles to keep her feet anchored. Next he secured her wrists to cuffs on either side of her body, and brought a thick strap over her midriff to hold her in place against the table. Reaching down, he pushed a button on the side of the table that caused the back of it to slowly lift until Carly's back was raised to a semi-upright position. Her legs were spread wide, her cunt and ass fully exposed on the edge of the padded table.

Adam moved to stand between Carly's knees. He reached toward the counter, selecting a tube of lubricant and a slim black dildo with a circular rubber base. He unwrapped the dildo and squirted a dollop of lubricant on its tip, wiping the excess lube against Carly's exposed asshole. He pressed the tip of the dildo against her entrance, easing it carefully into her. She felt a slight pressure as he pushed the base of the dildo into her. A moment later he flicked its battery on, sending a vibrating hum through her loins.

Next he unwrapped a flesh-colored dildo, this one substantially larger, and squirted lube over its head as well. He stroked her spread sex with two fingers, moving against her labia before sliding them inside her. After several moments he removed his fingers, replacing them with the large dildo. As it pressed its way inside her, Carly felt her vaginal muscles clamping around it.

From her semi-upright position she could see his erect cock outlined against his shorts and she experienced a sudden spasming ache in her cunt. She didn't want to be filled with rubber and plastic—she wanted Adam inside her. She didn't want to be strapped down and sexually tortured—she wanted to be in Adam's bed, in his arms, with his cock, thick and hard, sliding into her wetness as he kissed her mouth and whispered sweet things into her ear.

Stop it, she admonished herself.

Adam twisted the base of the phallus, bringing it to pulsing, vibrating life inside her cunt, sending whirling tremors of pleasure radiating through her body. He moved to stand beside her, reaching for her breasts.

"Pleasure," Adam said, as he tweaked her nipples, gently tugging and twisting them, "or what your brain might initially process as pleasure, can be as intense and as extreme as pain. Prolonged sexual stimulation can become a kind of torture in and of itself. Add the overlay of the enforced discipline of self-control and the erotic suffering can be raised to the sublime."

Carly was barely listening. All she knew was that she wanted to feel his mouth on her breasts. She wanted to taste his lips and his tongue with hers. She wanted it so much she nearly begged, only managing to stay quiet by pressing her lips tightly together and turning her head to the side, her eyes closed.

To her astonishment, she felt Adam leaning over her, his mouth closing over her right nipple, the nip of his teeth sending a jolt of red hot desire searing through her veins. She could feel the rasp of his unshaven jaw against her skin as he licked and teased her jutting nipple.

His fingers, still slick with lubricant, found their way to her spread cunt, stroking and lightly teasing the engorging flesh of her labia and the hard button of her clit aching for his touch.

Fuck. Carly felt her body begin to tremble, the telltale heat of a rising orgasm moving over her chest and throat. *No. No, no, no, no.* She stiffened, her muscles rigid, her eyes squeezed closed. *I will not come. I will not come.*

All at once his mouth was gone from her breast, his fingers lifted from her throbbing clit. A second later she felt a sudden, startling shock against her inner thigh and she squealed her surprise. Another shock on her mons, just above her swollen sex, made her scream. Her eyes flew open to see Adam holding the shock prod.

"Did you come?" he demanded.

"No! No, Sir. No," Carly gasped. And it was true. Though she'd been teetering on the edge of a powerful orgasm, the electric shocks had pulled her back sharply from the brink. The dildos continued to vibrate inside her, however, and her nipples ached for the return of Adam's touch.

Adam eyed her doubtfully for a moment but then nodded, setting the shock prod down on the counter. Leaning over her, he cupped her breasts in his hands, kneading the flesh, rolling her nipples with sure fingers.

Carly bit her lips to keep from moaning. When his fingers again found their way to her spread, vibrating cunt, she shuddered and tensed. She felt as if her body was flowing along a molten, seething river of pure delicious sensation. *Just flow with it,* she tried to tell herself. *Don't let it take you over.*

Adam lifted his head from her left nipple and moved so his mouth was by her ear. "Go on, girl," he said, his fingers again stroking her clit, "come for me. *Now.*"

At his words, Carly let herself slide over the waterfall at the end of the molten river of pleasure coursing through her body. Spasms racking her body, her vaginal muscles clamping tightly on the vibrator, her hips lifting against the restraint of the leather belt. It seemed to go on, and on, and on until finally she sagged back against the table, her heart thumping against her sternum, her breath coming in shallow gasps.

She wanted him to release her wrists and take the dildos from her body. She wanted to be gathered into his arms so she could hide her face against his chest and feel the beating of his heart against her cheek.

But that didn't happen.

Instead, Adam flicked something at the base of the vibrator inside her cunt, making it whir and pulse even faster than before. He swirled the tips of his fingers against her distended, throbbing clit and almost immediately she felt the rise of another climax gripping her.

"Oh god." The words were pulled from her lips before she realized she was speaking.

"Don't," Adam said in a warning tone. "Self control."

"Oh," she said, not in reply, but in an effort to obey him. His mouth closed again over her nipple, his tongue swirling, his lips caressing.

"Help me," she whispered, not sure who she was entreating or what form such help would take.

It was no good—the orgasm was hurtling toward her like a wave, inexorable and relentless.

Then came the shocks, sudden bursts of pain like bee stings along her inner thighs. One touched her nipple, exploding in a firework of agony. The orgasm receded like mist burned away by a flame.

"No! No, no, no!" Carly cried, writhing in her bonds. The prod touched her again, on her other nipple, and then, worst of all, directly on her clit. Carly screamed, a long, loud wail that subsided into a series of gasps as she felt something warm and wet glide over her tender, swollen labia.

Lifting her head, she saw Adam crouched between her legs, his dark hair obscuring his face. His tongue moved in soothing circles over her sex, his touch obliterating the shock of a moment before. A sound pushed from her throat, a whimpering mewl. Again an orgasm threatened to claim her and she began to shake. She clenched her hands into fists, digging her nails hard into her palms, squeezing her eyes tight as she fought the rising pleasure wrought by his tongue, coupled with the pulsing, vibrating fullness in her cunt and ass.

All at once Adam pulled away, reaching again for the prod. Carly wailed in frustration and fear as he lifted it, touching the tip to her wet, throbbing clit.

She screamed, jerking in her bonds, hitting the back of her head hard against the bondage table.

He was again between her legs, his lips gliding over her labia, his tongue swirling away the fiery sting caused a moment before by the prod. His big, strong hands were on her inner thighs, holding her, spreading her open in both a symbolic and real testament to his complete control over her body and her reactions.

It was too much—too much stimulation, too much pain, too much trapped, aching longing for something she could never have. She was trembling, her heart hammering against her ribs, her breath rasping, tears running down her face.

She began to cry, deep, shuddering sobs that tore through her even while Adam's lips and tongue and the feel of his strong hands gripping her dragged yet another deep, consuming orgasm from her exhausted body.

~*~

She tasted like honey and fresh rainwater with an underlay of exotic spice. He loved the feel of her shuddering body, the swell of her hard little clit against his tongue, the breathy orgasmic cries as she arched and writhed against him.

He loved the way she took a beating, her nipples engorging, her cheeks flushing, the way she leaned into the whip once she passed a certain point of resistance and surrendered herself to its kiss. He thrilled to her reactions with the prod—the way she startled and gasped, though her nipples remained as hard as small stones, fairly begging for his kiss.

He hadn't meant to lick her cunt, but its spicy-sweet scent had called to him, making his mouth water with the need to taste it once again. He reveled in his power and her reactions as he licked and teased his bound slave girl with his tongue. He wanted to lift his head, to tell her she could come, but he was lost in the taste of her, the feel of her, the sweet trembling of her body.

Then he heard the sound of her crying and he lifted his head, not sure at first what he was hearing. Tears were streaming from her tightly closed eyes, and her chest was heaving, not with orgasmic shudders, but with sobs. "Carly," he said in alarm, reaching up to stroke her wet cheek.

A part of him understood what was happening. She was on sensory overload—he'd taken her to that point where pleasure and pain not only merged, but became overwhelming sensation—too much to handle, too much to endure. Her crying was her release, a way for her body and mind to process the flood of sensation he had foisted on her.

But another part of him wondered—had he gone too far again? Had he violated the bond of innate trust between Dom and sub? Did such a bond even exist when the play was bought and paid for?

Quickly but carefully he turned off and removed the vibrators from Carly's orifices, setting them on the counter for later sterilization. He pulled the Velcro straps from her ankles and undid the bonds that held her body and wrists. He leaned over her, intending to scoop her into his arms and carry her to the sofa.

Before he could this, to his surprise she reached for him, wrapping her arms around his neck and pulling him down toward her. Her cheeks were hot and stained with tears.

"Please," she whispered against his ear. "Please."

That was all she said, just the single word, as she held him tight and hid her face against his neck. Adam's cock throbbed in his shorts, his balls aching with need. Without thinking through what he was doing, he reached for his fly. He jerked his shorts open and pushed them down his thighs, kicking them aside.

Carly's arms were still wrapped around his neck, her face hidden. Leaning over her, Adam positioned his hard cock between her legs and pressed into the grasping wetness. Her muscles pulled him in, hugging his shaft. Carly arched against him, her low primal groan igniting his passion to a fever pitch.

Adam brought his arms under her, pulling her up against his body, thrusting deeper inside her. Her cunt was so tight, gripping him like a wet velvet sheath, milking his cock as he moved inside her. She kept her arms tight around his neck as she undulated beneath him. He could feel her breasts crushed against his chest, the nipples stiff against his skin. He could feel the thud of her heart, or was it his, and feel the puff of her sweet breath as she gasped in time to his thrusts.

"Adam, oh Adam!" she cried softly. "Can I come? Oh please, Sir, may I?"

"Yes," he gasped. "Yes, do it. Come for me." Carly's cunt spasmed around his cock, sucking the hot jism from his cock and balls. He groaned, holding her tight against him until his own shudders subsided.

Their bodies were slick with sweat when he finally let her go and pushed himself to a standing position. She lay sprawled on the bondage table, her eyes closed, her long, wild curls like a lion's mane around her flushed face, her chest slowly rising and falling, her cunt glistening like a sticky, crushed orchid between her spread legs.

Adam stared at her for a long time, as the sweat cooled and dried on his body and his heart resumed its normal beat. He hadn't planned to fuck her. The intent—the purpose of this exercise was to break her down through sexual release—to force her into multiple orgasms and in so doing to take her deeper into sexual submission.

Instead he'd been the one enslaved—by her scent, the feel of her skin, the power of her reactions, the lure of her raw sexuality.

Adam Wise was not a man who fell in love. He'd been involved with a number of women over the years, all of them beautiful, all of them sophisticated, elegant and, he realized now, as cold and emotionally shut down as he was.

It was safer that way—that's what he'd always believed. It was cleaner too, less complicated, less draining. After his brief and disastrous marriage in his early twenties to a woman who'd ground his heart like glass beneath her heel, he'd vowed never again to let himself be ruled by his emotions or his cock.

This whole slave-for-hire situation had been ideal—no unrealistic expectations or illusions on either side. Both he and Carly knew just exactly what they were getting, and that was that. No strings, no messy emotional complications, no miscommunications or recriminations.

Okay, so what was the problem? Why did he feel so strange, so raw and vulnerable? He'd fucked her—so what? That was his prerogative. It was expected—it was part of the package. She was really little more than a kinky prostitute, when you got down to it—a very expensive kinky whore. Definitely not someone worthy of love.

Love!

Adam snorted at the absurd notion and stepped back, bending down to grab his shorts. "Carly," he said as he pulled them on. When she didn't respond, he snapped, "Carly! Look at me."

She opened her eyes and fixed them on his face. Closing her legs, she lifted herself to a sitting position. "Yes, Sir?"

"Did you come without permission during the exercise?"

"The...exercise?"

Adam saw the hurt in her eyes. He ignored it. "Answer the question."

A blush pinked her cheeks. "Yes, Sir. I'm sorry, Sir."

Adam nodded. "Like I said before—we've got time." He grinned, relieved to feel the uncomfortable tide of confused emotions draining away as he regained his control and came back to his senses. "Practice makes perfect."

Chapter 10

That night Carly lay wide-eyed in bed at Adam's feet, sleep eluding her. She couldn't get the memory of that afternoon's events out of her head. The shock play had been intense, pushing her past self-imposed boundaries and shaking her to her core. But that wasn't what was keeping her awake.

It was the physical memory of Adam's cock pulsing inside her, and the way he'd held her so tightly in his arms while he thrust and moaned over her. When she'd first signed up for the slave training, she'd been more than a little apprehensive about what it would be like to be fucked by a man she barely knew and most probably would have little attraction to. She'd talked herself into believing she could handle it, the dangling carrot of thirty-five thousand dollars waiting at the end of the month leading her forward.

She hadn't counted on Adam Wise or the feelings he had engendered in her. She hadn't expected her own deepening sense of connection to him as he took her further each day into a kind of submission she'd never experienced.

She could hear Adam's deep, even breathing and see the slow rise and fall of his chest in the glow of the moonlight streaming through the windows. She touched her lips, feeling the lack of his kiss. That was all that had been missing that afternoon — the press of his lips on hers, the interplay of their tongues as their bodies had moved in tandem.

Hadn't she always heard that prostitutes didn't kiss, but only fucked? That kissing was too intimate, too much an act of love versus the mere sexual transaction of copulation? And yet, if she were honest, she would have given anything for Adam's kiss when his cock had been inside her.

Clearly he hadn't been interested in that level of intimacy. Maybe he was incapable of it. Maybe he always bought the sex he needed, consciously avoiding any connection that might possibly move into something more intimate, something that might hurt him.

That was pretty pathetic, wasn't it? Why did she keep thinking these absurd romantic thoughts about a man who was incapable of any kind of meaningful relationship?

And yet…

When he'd dipped his head down between her legs, his tongue stoking the flames of her need, wasn't that in itself a supremely intimate act? And when Adam had gathered her into his arms, pulling her close as he moved inside her, that hadn't felt like some guy just getting his rocks off.

It had felt like a man making love.

Lifting her head, Carly turned her pillow over and punched it back into shape. It felt stupid and wrong to be sleeping at the foot of the bed. She should be up there beside him, curled into his strong arms, her head on his chest, her leg over his thighs…

What if…?

Did she dare?

Lifting her head again, she saw on the clock beside the bed that it was 2:46. She'd been tossing and turning for over three hours. This was insane. She just knew if she could lie beside him she would fall instantly asleep. And she could set her internal alarm, which never failed her, so she could wake up and move back down before he woke in the morning, none the wiser.

"Adam," she whispered, just in case he was a lighter sleeper than she thought. There was no reaction. She touched his leg through the blanket that separated them. He didn't move. Throwing off her own coverlet, she scooted slowly along the bed until she was beside him. Her heart was beating fast and she recognized this probably wasn't a good idea, but she was too keyed up and exhausted all at the same time to care.

She stayed still for several minutes, just watching his face, silvered by the moonlight. His thick lashes cast a shadow on his cheek and a lock of his dark hair had fallen over one eye.

Slowly, silently, she lifted the covers and slid her body down beside his. He was warm and solid, a comforting masculine presence that she didn't realize how much she had missed in the year since her last real relationship. Carefully she nestled her cheek in the crook of his arm, not quite daring to put her head on his chest, though she wanted to.

His breathing continued, slow and deep, and after several more minutes, she dared to put her arm over his body, snuggling closer. Her heart nearly stopped when he rolled toward her, his arms coming around her.

Adam sighed softly, but still seemed to be asleep. Gradually Carly relaxed in his embrace, her eyelids drooping, her mind emptying, her muscles easing. Just before she drifted to sleep, she leaned her face up to his and kissed his lips, just the lightest brush of skin on skin.

To her astonishment he kissed her back, pulling her closer, his lips parting, his tongue entering her mouth. She couldn't stop the urgent, sudden moan that filled her mouth, nor control the dance of her tongue against his. His hands moved over her back as they kissed, and she could feel the press of his erection against her thigh.

As suddenly as he'd embraced her, Adam moved away from her. He rolled onto his back, pulling Carly with him so that her head found its way to his chest. His breathing had again assumed its slow, even rise and fall. Had he really been asleep during that amazing kiss?

She could feel the steady, reassuring thump of his heart against her cheek, and while she could have kissed him all night, fatigue again stole over her, making her muscles limp and drawing her eyelids down. It felt so good, so *right*, to be in his arms. So what if he caught her there in the morning? Whatever punishment he decided to mete out would be worth these few hours of sweetness in the dark.

~*~

Something was tickling Adam's nose, pulling him from a sweet, warm dream. He twisted his head away from the tickle and then opened his eyes when he realized what it was. Carly's silky curls were in his face, her cheek warm on his chest, her body molded against his.

All at once the kiss came back to him, the kiss that, half asleep, he'd allowed himself to believe was part of a dream, though in his heart of hearts he'd known it was no dream.

Carly had defied him, breaking one of the rules he'd set out from the beginning—she was to sleep at the foot of his bed. Slaves did not curl up beside their

Masters, at least not the sort of slave he was interested in owning.

Or so he had told himself.

But that was before he'd made love to Carly on the bondage table. Before he'd tasted her spicy sweetness and felt the tight, perfect grip of her cunt around his cock.

Holy shit.

He was getting in too deep for comfort. It had been years since he'd felt this sort of attraction to a woman, the kind of attraction that he well knew could be his undoing. He would fall for her and even if she stayed with him when the month was done, he would never know, not for certain, that she was there because she cared for him, or because she liked the free meal ticket and roof over her head.

The very nature of their strange liaison assured that it had to end when the month was done. Anything else would be fraught with potential pain and disillusionment, and he'd had enough of that to last a lifetime, thank you.

Pushing the sleeping girl from him, he yawned loudly and turned over, his back to her. A moment later he felt her scrambling down to where she should have been in the first place. He lay still for a long time, letting his thoughts drift and slowly easing back into a light sleep.

He was awakened by her burrowing beneath the covers, this time to seek out and suck his cock. As he let her lick and stroke him, he decided not to say anything about her infraction. It would just muddy the waters. Better to leave it be and pretend it had never happened.

~*~

All day Monday Adam put Carly through her paces, barely giving her a chance to catch her breath. As the minutes and hours ticked by, Carly kept waiting for him to say something about what she had done, certain her punishment would be severe, but he never said a word.

He bound her from head to foot in rope, leaving only her cunt and ass exposed. She was blindfolded and suspended horizontally from the dungeon ceiling beam, sexually teased and tortured for hours, after which he spanked both her ass and cunt until she both orgasmed and cried, in the end not sure if the pleasure or the pain had gotten the best of her.

She barely had the strength to eat the dinner he fed her. She was grateful when he let her soak in the tub and go to bed early. Almost the moment she lay down at the foot of the bed, sleep had dropped over her exhausted body like a curtain.

When Carly woke up early Tuesday morning, she realized she'd never even heard Adam come to bed. Lifting herself on one elbow, she watched the sleeping man for several minutes, still musing about the stolen kisses two nights before and whether he even remembered or knew it had happened.

After her morning shower and grooming, Carly stood at attention, arms behind her head, waiting for Adam's daily inspection of her body. He came into the bedroom a moment later, his cell phone in hand. He looked unhappy. "I had planned to take the whole week off, but I got a call just now while you were in the shower. There's a problem at one of the subsidiaries in the city and I need to get down there and put out a few fires. I'll probably be gone for at least five hours."

Carly realized she didn't want him to go. She found herself annoyed that Adam's business, whatever it was, couldn't take care of itself for one freaking day without him, but of course she held her tongue on the matter.

Pocketing the phone, Adam ran his fingers over Carly's body, sending a shiver of desire through her that she struggled to contain. He seemed distracted, even when he marked her ass with the whip.

As they walked down the stairs, Adam continued, "I don't want to leave you idle for too long while I'm gone. After your regular chores, there's a closet in my study I've been meaning to clean out for months. No need to wear your French maid outfit, since I won't be here to see you."

They entered the study together. Adam moved toward the closet in question, pulling open the folding doors. "I don't want the cleaning crew to get their hands in here because they like to throw everything away and I'm something of a pack rat. I'll show you what I want done after breakfast. Then I've got to hit the road before the rush hour traffic gets too insane."

Carly looked around Adam's study, taking in the furnishings and the pictures on the walls. It was a masculine room, all dark leather and polished wood. A faded Oriental carpet covered most of the hardwood floor. There was a large mahogany desk with a gold pen set in a marble base and a sleek looking laptop on the polished surface. Framed photographs lined the walls, most of them of Adam shaking hands with various dignitaries, politicians and movie stars, many of them in front of office buildings with the words *Wise Subsidiaries* engraved in brass and stone. Carly made a mental note to do a Google search on the company, and on Adam himself, maybe even later that morning if she had a chance.

Carly realized as she thought this that she hadn't had access to a computer or a cell phone since she'd signed up for the slave training at the auction house. She thought about the countless hours she used to waste on Facebook, YouTube, and at various BDSM porn sites. She realized now that she didn't miss any of that, not a bit.

Glancing at the antique pendulum clock on the mantle, she noted it was already after nine. She'd completed her upstairs chores and now it was time to focus on the task at hand. She moved resolutely toward the closet. Adam hadn't been kidding about being a packrat. There were dozens of boxes piled one on top of the other on the floor of the closet, and more boxes stuffed into the shelves that lined the space. There were plastic folders stuffed with papers and boxes of unopened office supplies.

"I admit it's mostly junk—old receipts, Christmas cards, letters from family members, several boxes of old photos I haven't looked at in a hundred years," Adam had said when he'd showed her the closet. "There are even some old VHS tapes I used to keep around for my nephews, and other crap I don't even remember. What I'd like you to do is organize it into some kind of order. I have some plastic bins I bought for the project, but I just never quite get the time to make it happen. Just do the best you can and sort the stuff into some kind of logical order in the bins. Don't throw anything out. I'll look it over when I get a chance. Think you can handle that?"

"Yes, Sir. I was an office manager and administrative assistant in a law office. I have a very organized mind."

"Excellent. I'll see you later today. When you're done with the closet, you can do what you like—take a bath, take a nap, whatever." Reaching into the pocket of the sports jacket he was wearing, he had handed her a cell phone. "I'm going to call you when I'm ten minutes from the house. I will expect to find you kneeling in the front hall, your forehead on the floor, arms in front of you, ass in the air, when I get home. Is that clear?"

"Yes, Sir."

Now Carly took the six colored plastic bins he'd brought into the study after breakfast. She lined them up on the desk and then took out a box. She began to sort through receipts, Broadway playbills and business correspondence from someone named Nathan Wise to various vendors and suppliers, none dated more recently than 1993. She decided Nathan must be Adam's father, and wondered what he was like. What family did Adam have? Was he, or had he once been married?

There were two boxes of VHS tapes, many of them Disney movies and cartoons. She realized she knew next to nothing about Adam Wise, not even if he had kids. This closet, she realized, was an opportunity to learn more about him, even if that hadn't been his intention.

And yet, she thought as she reached for a box that contained a jumble of old photographs, maybe it *had* been his intention, at least on some level. Why else give her access to a part of his private life? Finally she found a box that was of personal interest to her. Inside were photos of family members, or so she guessed. Various Adams ranging in age from his early twenties to the present were in many of them, waving and smiling against gorgeous beach backdrops or snowy-peaked mountains, or leaning with the casual nonchalance of the very wealthy against the hood of some incredibly expensive looking automobile.

At the back of the closet she found an old trumpet in a musty case, and what looked like an Eagle Scout sash, covered with faded embroidered merit badges, including an open-mouthed snake, a swimmer's lifebelt, a campfire, a compass, a pine tree, a red cross, a canoe and half a dozen others, all neatly stitched onto the wide, faded green sash. Carly closed her eyes, trying to imagine Adam as a Boy Scout, working hard to earn each badge, always prepared.

She sorted through the photos, neatening them into piles and placing them in precise stacks in one of the bins. One photo in particular caught her eye and she stopped to study it. It was Adam, a younger Adam—he barely looked to be out of his teens. Beside him stood a beautiful young woman with ice-blue eyes, tall and slender, her white-blond hair piled in an elaborate twist intertwined with silk ribbons, her long, lithe body draped in a heavy satin wedding gown with seed pearls beaded over the bodice. Adam, his hair curling nearly to his shoulders, was grinning broadly beside her, his head angled in her direction, dressed in a tuxedo with a red satin cummerbund, a red rose pinned to his lapel.

Carly leaned against the desk, studying the picture. So Adam *had* been married! That wasn't so surprising—most people got married at some point, why not a handsome, wealthy guy like Adam Wise?

The question was, where was this woman now?

Carly had just assumed Adam wasn't presently married—there was no sign of a woman in the house as far as she could see, nor could she imagine a wife who would permit her husband to bring home a sex slave for a month while she discreetly melted into the background, no matter what kind of relationship they had. Adam wore no ring, nor was there any telltale tan line or subtle indentation on his ring finger that indicated he had merely removed the evidence of his marital status.

More than that, he didn't have the *feel* of a married man, which, unfortunately, Carly was all too aware of, having once had the very bad judgment to fall for one of the married attorneys in her office. Married men carried themselves differently. While Carly might have been hard pressed to define it precisely, they were marked in a way single men were not.

No, she told herself firmly, Adam was definitely single.

So what had happened to cause him to divorce? There were so many questions she wanted to ask him, so much she wanted to know about this man who was basically a mystery to her, beyond the fact that he had once been married, had been a Boy Scout, was insanely rich, too handsome for his own good, and the best Dom she'd ever been with or known, not to mention an amazing lover.

She grinned at herself, imagining what her best friend Donna would say when she told her all she knew about the guy was that he was rich, handsome and a great lover.

"So what else do you need to know?" Donna would have demanded, laughing. "When's the wedding?"

Carly stared again at the photo of the newlyweds, noting that it was Adam who was turned toward his bride, while she stared into the camera, something in her expression cool, even aloof, on the day that should have been her happiest.

Carly thought about the idea of the lover and the beloved—how one person was the object of the other's love and accepted it as their due, while ultimately being unable, or unwilling, to return it in kind. Most relationships were like that, Carly thought—with one person more invested than the other, turning their face and their heart toward the beloved, who looks straight ahead, their eyes already on a future that doesn't include the lover, even if neither of them knows it yet.

Carly placed the photo into the bin.

Was that what was happening now between her and this man she could never know?

"Adam," she whispered with a sigh, angrily brushing away a tear.

Chapter 11

Carly was standing in front of the sofa, naked save for her red leather collar. Her arms were behind her back, each hand gripping the opposite elbow. Adam, James and Amy were sitting together sipping glasses of wine, Adam on the chair, James on the sofa with Amy kneeling on the carpet beside him, her cheek resting on his knee as she gazed up at him with a serene look of utter contentment. Something about Amy's expression caught at Carly's heart, filling her with longing.

When Adam had told her the couple was coming over that evening, Carly hadn't been sure what to expect. He'd explained they were husband and wife, as well as Master and slave, but he hadn't mentioned anything about the radiance that seemed to bounce between them, a kind of light that shone from their eyes whenever they looked at each other.

Was that love?

Carly had been in love before. Well, perhaps not precisely in love, but in intense and lustful attraction that had masqueraded as love, at least for a while. She'd lived with three different men over the years, two of them into BDSM on the dominant side of the equation, or what she had thought of as dominant, though neither of them came close to Adam's level of intensity and control.

Looking back on those failed relationships, Carly realized she had been able to manipulate each man into doing what she wanted, or what she had thought she wanted, but in the process she'd lost the respect and passion she now understood was necessary for a D/s relationship to be sustainable. Adam wasn't a man who could be manipulated, but nor was he a man who would have looked at her twice outside of this artificial construct.

Okay, so what? We've already established that, Carly, so get over it. Even though she knew there was no potential for anything past these thirty days of play, that didn't mean that Carly didn't want to please her temporary Master, especially in front of Amy and James.

Though she'd only been with Adam a few days, she already felt a kind of loyalty toward him that came to the fore now that there were witnesses. She wanted to make him proud, and even more importantly, she wanted to prove to herself that she could obey and serve him as the trained slave she professed to be. Silently she promised herself that no matter what was asked of her tonight, she would submit with all the grace and obedience she possessed.

"Carly handles erotic pain well," Adam was saying. "She is meticulous in doing her chores. She's eager to please."

"But...?" James said, his eyes twinkling. He was probably in his early sixties, Carly guessed, with a thick mane of silver hair brushed back from a high forehead, the lines radiating from corners of his eyes and the brackets around his mouth suggesting a man who laughed often. He wasn't precisely handsome — his deep set eyes were too close on either side of a nose that was too big for his face, but there was a kindness and peace in his expression that made him attractive. "I hear a definite *but* in that statement."

Adam laughed. "Orgasm control. She's definitely lacking in that area, right, Carly?"

Carly felt the heat move over her skin and knew she was blushing. "Yes, Sir," she admitted, stealing a glance at Amy, who no doubt could climax from a puff of air on her cunt, or withstand hours of sexual stimulation until given permission by her Master to let herself go.

Amy was beautiful by any reckoning, despite being over sixty. Her hair was also silver, and cut short around a pixie face. She had large, doe-like eyes a rich shade of golden-brown, and a full mouth, also bracketed by smile lines. Her cheeks dimpled when she smiled, which she was doing now.

"Remember our first year, James?" Amy said, as she looked over at Carly. "I had the control of a three-year-old and the patience of a gnat." James grinned and nodded, stroking her head. Amy turned to look at Adam. "Carly's had, what, a few days with you?"

Adam looked sheepish. "That about sums it up. Though she is a trained professional," he added with a small frown.

"Nevertheless," Amy continued, smiling toward Carly, who returned a grateful glance, "it takes time to get used to a new Master. I'd say she's doing pretty well, wouldn't you agree, James?"

"I would indeed." Turning to Adam, James said, "I brought along my new bullwhip." He pointed toward a hard leather case he had set down beside the couch. "Amy got it for me, or should I say for herself" — he grinned, winking at his wife — "when we were in Australia. It's made from kangaroo hide and packs a powerful wallop, right, slave girl?"

"Yes, *Sir*." Amy grinned back at him.

"Maybe we can test out your claim of Carly's ability to handle pain. What do you think, Adam?"

"I think it's an excellent idea," Adam replied. He turned to Carly. "That is, if it's all right with you. Have you experienced a bullwhip before?"

"No, Sir," Carly replied. "But I've watched demonstrations." She liked the way Adam was around his friends. Something in his demeanor was gentler and more solicitous of her. It was like a bridge between their stolen, unspoken kisses in the night, and the stern taskmaster he presented during the day.

Which of the Adams was the real one?

She turned to James. "I think I could handle it, Sir." She'd never been with someone skilled enough to use a bullwhip and was aware it took special training and technique. Somehow she knew James would have that skill, and she realized she already trusted the man completely, though she'd only known him for an hour. This would be her chance to prove her obedience and masochistic grace. She made a silent promise not to let Adam, or herself, down.

James rose from the couch. "I think you could too." He reached for the case and set it on the couch, undoing the clasps and opening the lid. He withdrew a short-handled bullwhip of dark brown leather, its plaited thong easily six feet long and tapering to a wicked-looking cracker at its end.

"We wouldn't want Amy to feel left out," he said, reaching a hand down to his wife. "How about we'll string up the girls side-by-side? That suit you, my darling slave girl?"

"Oh, yes," Amy breathed, her eyes shining as she took the offered hand.

Amy wore a silky dress that clung to her small, narrow frame. She slipped out of it without a trace of self-consciousness. While no doubt not as pert as they once were, her small breasts were still pretty, the nipples pierced with golden hoops. She had a thatch of silver pubic hair between her legs, neatly trimmed and shaved into the shape of a heart. As she turned, Carly saw she had a tattoo just above her small ass. The design was a silver chain entwined with small pink roses, the words *James' Girl* written in black lettering just below it.

Adam and James led the two women to the central beam from which chains and cuffs hung waiting. Carly wasn't sure whether to feel grateful or competitive with the older woman, and realized she felt a little of both. *She's had decades of training*, Carly reminded herself. *Just do your own personal best.*

As the men positioned and cuffed them, Amy leaned her head close to Carly and whispered with an encouraging smile, "James is wonderful with a bullwhip. Just let yourself flow with the pain—let it take you to that special place."

James started slowly, using a flogger at first to warm and sensitize their skin. Carly closed her eyes, reveling in the thuddy strokes of the leather, almost like an embrace as they brushed her skin. As the flogging progressed, Carly's breath quickened to a pant. She felt her cunt moistening and opened her eyes, seeking out Adam. She couldn't see him and realized he must be standing behind her. Amy had her eyes closed, her lips lifted in a small, serene smile.

After a time James said, "I'll be switching to the whip now, girls. Amy, what's your safeword?"

"Rose, Sir," she replied, not a trace of breathlessness in her voice.

"And you, Carly?"

Carly drew in and then let out a long breath in an effort to slow her breathing. "Auction."

"Good. Remember, there's no shame in using your safeword. It's a tool, a way of communicating that can be essential, especially when folks are just getting comfortable with each other. No one will judge you if you use it. It's not a sign of weakness." He paused while Carly absorbed this and then added, "And if you find you can't speak? What do you do then, Amy?"

"Make a fist and then open and close my hand, Sir."

"That's right. Same goes for you, Carly, got it?"

"Yes, Sir."

The loud cracking sound of the bullwhip made Carly jump, her gasp audible. Amy remained perfectly still beside her. When it popped again, Amy moved slightly, and Carly realized the whip had made contact. Another crack, and this time it was Carly who jumped even before her brain processed the sudden, stinging welt left by the tip of the whip on her ass.

Over and over the whip cracked first against Amy's ass and then Carly's. Though she tried to steel herself, each time the tip made contact with her skin,

Carly jerked and gasped. Amy remained still as a graceful statue beside her, though her head began slowly to fall back, her lips parting.

Each cracking pop of leather against her ass left a small trail of blazing heat. Carly began to dance on her toes, her body twisting to avoid the lash, even as her mind ordered it to stay still and deal. It hurt, oh, it hurt! Carly's heart beat fast and high in her throat. Her ass felt like it was on fire as the whip snaked again and again over her skin.

Auction. I can say the word and they'll stop. They won't judge me. It's not a sign of weakness.

Suddenly she felt a hand on her back, and Adam's voice near her ear, his tone soothing. "Stop fighting it, Carly. Flow with it. Flow with the pain. Embrace it. Accept it. Breathe. Take long, deep breaths. I know you can do this."

Carly leaned back into his touch, feeling as if he'd just pulled her back from the brink of giving up. She *could* do this. She *was* doing it. She was grateful for his words and determined to do better.

Taking as much air into her lungs as she could, Carly slowly exhaled, and then drew in another slow breath. The cracking of the bullwhip continued, but this time when it touched her skin, Carly forced herself to lean into the pain, to reach for it. It hurt as much as it had before, but somehow she was able to handle it better. Adam's words still echoed inside her head—*I know you can do this.*

Carly glanced at Amy, who remained still and serene beside her, her head back, a look of utter peace on her face. Carly let her own eyes close and dropped her head back too, as if by assuming the position, she would find the same level of serenity and acceptance.

"Yes," she heard Adam breathe softly behind her. "Yes, that's it. Good girl. I'm proud of you."

Something began to shift inside her. She didn't feel precisely serene, but she found she could tolerate the fiery sting. Not only tolerate it, her skin actually tingled in anticipation of the lash as she waited her turn to feel its cracking kiss. She fantasized it was Adam wielding the whip, and they were alone. Soon he would take her down and make love to her, his skin cool against her fire, his kiss soothing away the pain...

She realized the whipping had stopped, and some kind of soothing balm was being gently stroked over her stinging, abraded skin. And then the cuffs were released, and Adam had his arm around her shoulders. He led her to the sofa, where Amy was already kneeling in front of James, who sat back, the bullwhip curled on his lap.

"Very impressive," James said, smiling at Carly. "Adam didn't exaggerate your grace in handling erotic pain."

Carly found herself beaming back at James, a sense of pride making her feel warm and happy. James looked at Adam and asked, "What else did you have in mind for this evening?"

"I was thinking we should give Carly a turn in the cock box. She's quite skilled in pleasing a man with her mouth. I know she'd be honored to show you, James. Isn't that right, slave girl?"

The warmth and happiness that had suffused Carly a moment before shriveled into a hard ball in her stomach as she stared at the wooden chest with the glory holes drilled into the sides. She hadn't told Adam of her fear of small spaces. Even a crowded elevator was sometimes enough to send her into panic mode. How would she cope with being placed in that narrow coffin-like structure? What if she started screaming, or worse?

All three of them were looking at her expectantly, Amy and James smiling, Adam with his eyebrows raised, his head slightly cocked, as if looking to her for confirmation.

I'm proud of you.

Adam's words played in her head as the three of them waited for her response. She couldn't let him down. How hard could it be to lie in the box for a few minutes? She would have the distraction of the men's cocks to suck and pleasure. Adam was right—she *was* good at that, and she knew it.

"Yes, Sir," she said, pushing past the hoarseness that threatened in her voice.

James and Adam removed the thick padding from the top of the chest. The lid was closed by clasps along one side, which they released. When they lifted the lid, Carly could see that inside it was lined with a thick quilt and there was even a small pillow for her head. She would just pretend she was in a bed in the dark. That was all. She'd keep her eyes closed and use her hands and her mouth to pleasure her Masters. It would be easy.

No sweat.

She could do this.

She accepted Adam's hand when he offered it, stepping gingerly into the narrow space. Swallowing hard over the lump that had risen suddenly in her throat, Carly lowered herself onto the soft quilt and lay back, forcing the bubbles of panic threatening to burst through her to stay down, compressed into the small ball of anxiety still twisting in her gut.

When the lid closed, she shut her eyes. The sound of the latches closing with metallic finality caused a rush of foul tasting bile to rise in her throat. She swallowed again, willing herself to be calm. She could hear the muffled sound of masculine voices, and a moment later she felt the brush of a cock head against her cheek.

She turned her face toward the phallus, recognizing Adam's scent and girth as her lips closed over the shaft. There was a sound on the other side and she turned her head to find what must be James' cock, longer and thinner than Adam's, but just as hard. Tentatively she licked a circle around the head. He tasted clean and she took more of the shaft into her mouth, while maneuvering to reach Adam's offered shaft with her hand.

That's when she made her mistake.

She opened her eyes.

The box was black as pitch inside and all at once it felt as if the wooden walls were closing in on her. The twisting ball of anxiety she'd kept at bay in her gut hurtled through her body, turning the blood in her veins to ice and making her feel sick and lightheaded, as if she was going to pass out.

She tried to concentrate on what she was doing, but her mouth had gone dry, her tongue sticking to the roof of her mouth, her teeth chattering. Her heart was thundering in her chest and she couldn't seem to catch her breath. Her body was slicked with sweat, a rank vinegar smell coming from under her arms.

Safeword. I have a safeword. Say the fucking safeword.

She opened her mouth, but no sound came. She opened and closed her hands, but of course no one could see what she was doing. Panic took over the last vestiges of conscious, rational thought, dragging Carly along in the wake of it. She began to thrash, barely aware of what she was doing, desperate to escape, sure she was about to die...

~*~

Adam and James met each other's eye when they heard the scuffling sounds coming from the cock box. Something wasn't right. Before either could react, Amy, who had been kneeling submissively nearby, leaped to her feet. "Open the box. Something's wrong!"

James and Adam both pulled away from the chest. The latches were on James' side, and he moved quickly, releasing them and throwing back the lid. Carly was curled inside, her eyes squeezed shut, her face pale as death, twitching and thrashing as if she were having an epileptic seizure.

Panic gripped Adam's innards as he stared down at the girl. Amy pushed him aside and reached down, hauling Carly to a sitting position. "Help me get her out of there," she barked, no trace of submission in her tone. "She's having a panic attack. Why the hell did you let her do this?"

"I didn't know!" Adam cried. Together he and James lifted the shaking girl from the cock box and set her on the sofa. Her face was pale, her skin clammy to the touch.

Amy sat beside her, placing a hand on Carly's arm. "Carly, listen to me, sweetheart. It's okay. You're out of the box. You're safe. It's okay. You're okay." She stroked Carly's arm. Her voice was calm and reassuring, and Adam offered a silent prayer of thanks that there was a doctor here dealing with this situation.

Jesus! A panic attack! How the hell was he supposed to have known Carly didn't like confined spaces? Why hadn't she told him? Why hadn't it been in the hard limits section of the contract? Damn it, this wasn't his fault.

Was it?

"Breathe," Amy was saying. "Slow, deep breaths. We'll do it together. In, one, two..." She inhaled. "And out, one, two. Yes, that's it. One, two...nice and slow. You're safe now, Carly. You're doing good, baby. Breathe."

Adam was intensely relieved to see Carly relaxing against the sofa back. Her shaking had subsided and the color had returned to her face. He glanced at James, who had pulled his jeans back on, and realized he himself was still naked, his cock flaccid. He grabbed his underwear and jeans, pulling them on.

Bending down, he held out Amy's dress to her, but Amy waved it away. "Not now," she mouthed. Aloud she said, "Adam, can you get Carly a glass of water, please?"

Glad to have something to do, Adam raced from the dungeon. He poured a glass of water in the bathroom, and grabbed his robe on the way out.

When he returned to the dungeon, Carly was leaning forward on the sofa, her hands caught between her knees. There were tears on her face, but she seemed to be breathing normally, thank god, and her eyes were focused.

Adam handed her the glass of water, which she took, offering him a tremulous smile. Sitting on her other side, he draped his robe over her shoulders. "I'm so sorry," he said, his voice catching. "I didn't know."

"It's my fault," she whispered. "I should have told you. I thought I could handle it." Another tear slipped down her cheek.

"Carly, it's okay," Amy said in a firm but gentle tone, still in doctor mode. "Really it is. You had a panic attack. It can happen to anyone and it can come on suddenly. The fact you worked through it so quickly is an excellent sign. If you don't mind, I'd like to get my bag from the car and give you a quick examination, just to make sure everything's okay with you. And then you'll rest and take it easy. All right?"

Carly rocked forward, hugging herself. "Oh, gosh. I'm okay, really. I'm embarrassed is all—"

"No," Adam interrupted. "Let her, Carly. *Please.*"

Carly looked at Adam, her blue eyes wide, another tear slipping down her soft cheek.

A mistake, he realized with sudden, stark clarity. *This is all a mistake. What the hell was I thinking? You can't buy submission, for god's sake. This is my fault. My fault. I have to make this right. I have to stop this now.*

I have to let her go.

Chapter 12

There was no air in the tiny box. She could feel the pressure on all sides and knew it was a matter of minutes, maybe seconds, before the weight of the water crushed the box and it came pouring in. She might be able to hold her breath for a minute, maybe longer, and then, her lungs bursting, she would have no choice but to open her mouth, her silent screams drowned in a rush of saltwater...

"Carly! Carly, wake up. You're dreaming. Wake up!"

Carly felt herself being pulled upward — the blackness turning to green and then gold as she burst into the light. Gasping, she shook her head, gulping in the fresh, pure air.

It took several more seconds to realize she wasn't afloat in the ocean, but lying in a warm, safe bed. Adam loomed over her, his face a mask of concern. "You were talking in your sleep. Crying out. Are you okay?" He was sitting on the edge of the bed, dressed in shorts and a T-shirt, backlit by the light streaming in from the hall.

Carly pushed the hair from her face and tried to sit up, but fell back against the pillows, dizziness assailing her. She shuddered, the nightmare still clinging to her like a spider's sticky web. "It felt so real. I was in a box—"

"Shh, don't relive it. Let it go." Adam stroked the hair from her face. "This is all my fault. I'm so sorry, Carly. I didn't know."

Adam's words burned away the clammy fear left by the nightmare, his touch as warm as the sun. Carly smiled. "It's okay," she whispered, putting her hand over his. If the terrifying moments spent in the cock box had broken through whatever roadblocks had been erected between them by the nature of their strange relationship, then they had been worth it.

"It wasn't in the hard limits section of the contract," Adam added, pulling his hand away, his words hitting her like a slap in the face.

"The contract," Carly repeated stupidly. No. No, no, no. She wanted to scream, to grab him by the shirt and make him understand. Make him care. Instead she lay there, passive and tongue-tied.

Oblivious to the pain his words had caused her, Adam continued, "I've been up all night thinking about it, Carly. We can't keep doing this. It's not working out."

"I'm sorry, Sir?" Carly forced herself to sit up, pushing through the thick ooze of molasses that seemed to be surrounding her brain from the sedative

Amy had given her the night before. What was he saying? What wasn't working out? Whatever it was, she would fix it. She had to fix it. Pushing down the tendrils of panic creeping along her innards, she said breathlessly, "I can do better, I promise—"

Adam reached for her hand. "No, no—it isn't you, Carly. It's the situation itself. It's artificial—it's a game. I thought it was what I wanted, but I realize now, what I was doing is wrong. I don't think either of us had a real understanding of what we were getting into with the terms of the contract we'd negotiated. I just used you, like a toy, like an object. I didn't think about the trust that's necessary in this kind of a situation, or the potential danger. It has to end."

I used you — like a toy, like an object.

Adam was sending her away. She was nothing more than a toy. A toy he was tired of playing with. She meant nothing to him. She never had.

Carly tried to harness the righteous indignation rising inside her, but it didn't work. She felt as if she'd been sucker punched, all the air smacked from her lungs. Was that really all that mattered to Adam? The terms of some stupid contract? Had Carly been totally fooling herself that something more had been developing between them?

She pressed her lips together, blinking her eyes rapidly to keep back the tears that threatened to spill. What the hell did she expect? He'd *purchased* her at a slave auction, for god's sake. What kind of a man did that, anyway? The kind who couldn't or wouldn't make an emotional connection. The kind she would be smart to steer well clear of.

But there was more at stake here. She'd bet everything she had on this gig—the money she stood to earn would help her get back on her feet. Everything she owned was crammed into her crappy old car, parked and waiting in the lot behind the auction house. Now this rat bastard was going to ruin it, just like that.

Carly tried to focus on the terms of the stupid contract—to speak a language Adam could understand. "You can't send me away. Not before the contract ends. The money—"

"Don't worry about the money," Adam interrupted. "You'll get everything due you, I promise. If necessary, I'll put in the call myself."

She tried again. "If you report dissatisfaction, the contract will be void. I won't get a dime."

Adam shrugged. "I won't report a thing. I told you—you aren't the problem. It's me. I just—I can't do this. You don't have to finish the month. As soon as the sun's up, I'll have Jordan, my driver, take you wherever you want to go."

"But—"

"No buts. I've made my decision."

Desperate, she wouldn't give up, despite her rising humiliation at having to beg. "Please, it hasn't even been a week. I can—"

Adam put two fingers against her lips, silencing her. "Not bad money for less than a week's work, huh?"

Closing her eyes, Carly turned her head away.

~*~

"I'm sorry, what?"

"I said, where can I take you, ma'am? I need an address."

They were sitting in the circular driveway of the old brownstone, the engine idling, Carly in the backseat, Jordan waiting patiently for her reply. It was barely seven in the morning, but Carly hadn't wanted to linger a second longer than she had to in Adam's house. His words still burned inside her.

Not bad money for less than a week's work.

If she'd had any lingering doubt of Adam's real feelings, he'd made them crystal clear with that snide, heartless remark. What a fool she had been to think there had been something happening between them. What a clueless, naive fool. The innocent, sweet man gazing with such open love at his bride in the photo she had found had no doubt died a long time ago, leaving the cold, emotionally unavailable man that Adam Wise was today.

Carly hadn't seen Adam's driver since that first night when he'd driven them from the city. Jordan had been a witness to her orgasm in the back seat, though from his polite, blank expression, you'd think he'd never seen her before in his life. No doubt she was just the latest in a string of expendable girl toys Adam Wise had purchased for his amusement.

Where the hell did she tell him to go? If Donna were in town, she'd tell the driver to go there, but Donna was in New Zealand as a visiting professor at the University of Auckland. She couldn't very well tell Jordan to drive her to Miami, where her mother now resided with her third husband, a man who had made it very clear Carly wasn't welcome, unless she was willing to put herself up in a hotel. She couldn't go back to the girls she'd roomed with in Brooklyn, nor did she want to.

"Back to the auction house, please."

"Yes, ma'am." The sedan purred down the driveway. Carly resisted the urge to turn back to see if Adam was watching. Fuck Adam Wise and the horse he rode in on. If he didn't want her around, she damn well didn't want to be there.

What would they think at the auction house when she showed up more than three weeks early? Adam had said she would be paid, but what if there was some fine print in the contract that left her shit out of luck? Just because they kept his payment, that didn't mean she would necessarily get her share.

Carly stared out the window feeling numb as they drove along the highway, her limbs heavy, her mind a jumble of confused thoughts that refused to come into any kind of cohesive focus. Hot tears were creating a pressure behind her eyes, but she refused to give them permission to fall.

Carly sat up straighter, pressing her lips together, willing herself to be strong. No matter what happened, she'd pull herself up by her bootstraps and start over. She would leave New York—there was nothing keeping her there anyway. Whether or not she got the payout from the auction house she'd hit the road and never look back. There had to be jobs somewhere in the country—maybe down south or out west. If her old junk heap of a car could make it that far, she'd just start driving and not stop until she got there—wherever *there* happened to be.

Footloose and fancy free. That was the new Carly Abrams. No ties, no strings, no one to miss her when she'd gone.

"Are you okay, ma'am?"

Looking up, Carly saw Jordan's eyes in the rearview mirror. "I'm fine," she replied automatically. She touched her cheek, startled to realize it was streaked with tears.

~*~

Adam felt like he was made of stone. He stared out the window, seeing nothing, his mind's eye focused solely on the image of Carly standing in the front hall early that morning dressed in a white blouse and blue jeans, her suitcase beside her, her big blue eyes filled with tears. Had he made a mistake in sending her away so precipitously? Should he have tried to make it work?

He thought back to their conversation, which had been running in a loop in the back of his head since Jordan had driven her away. Carly's focus had been on the money. She hadn't said a word about anything else, her only concern apparently whether or not she would get paid if the contract was terminated before the month was out.

Yes, he told himself for the hundredth time. He'd done the right thing, made the right decision. He'd learned a lesson—now he would move on.

But was he being honest? Had he even given her a chance to speak? Was he so intent on his own agenda, his own issues, that he had shut her down before giving her a chance?

But she's gone now, he reminded himself. *It's for the best. It's for the best. It's for the best.* Maybe if he said it enough, it would actually be true.

The doorbell rang. Reflexively Adam looked at his watch. It was only eight o'clock. The cleaning crew wasn't due for several hours and Jordan wouldn't ring the bell — he had a key to the back door if he needed anything.

Pushing himself upright, Adam left his study and headed toward the front door. Peering through the peephole, he saw James and Amy standing on the stoop, Amy's black medical bag in her hand.

It wasn't like them to just show up, not that he minded. He pulled open the door. "Hey there. Is everything all right?"

"Everything's great." James replied with a smile. "I called first, but it went to voicemail. I hope we aren't disturbing you and Carly, but Amy was worried when you didn't call back. We just wanted to make sure everything's okay."

"Oh, sorry. I guess I left the phone up in the bedroom. I didn't realize you'd called."

"How's Carly?" Amy said, as Adam stepped back to let them in. "Can I see her?"

"She's not here."

"I'm sorry, what?" Amy, who had already been heading toward the stairs, stopped and turned to face Adam.

"She left."

"She left?" James echoed.

"Yeah. I had Jordan take her wherever she wanted to go."

"She wanted to leave?" James said.

"I didn't ask her. You saw what happened last night. I did what I had to do."

"You didn't *ask* her?" Amy dropped the medical bag and put her hands on her hips.

Adam found himself resenting Amy's critical tone. "Damn it, no! It wasn't something up for debate." He turned to James, not wanting to meet Amy's gaze. "You were right from the beginning, James. I got in way over my head with this. It was best to cut my losses and move on."

"Your losses!" Amy replied, as if he'd been addressing her. "Let me get this straight. Less than twelve hours ago this woman suffered a panic attack that required sedation. Clearly being put in that box was a trigger for her, and one she was probably aware of."

"Listen to me," Adam began but Amy cut him off.

"No, you listen to me, Adam Wise. James and I were talking about it, and Carly definitely hesitated when you suggested the cock box. At the time we just thought she was shy about the idea of servicing two men, but looking back, it was clear she was afraid. Yet she pushed past that fear because she wanted to please you. She wanted to obey you, Adam. She put her own issues aside in an effort to do that —"

"She was being paid good money to do that—" Adam interrupted, stung at Amy's criticism, which hurt all the more because he knew it was true.

"Forget the money for once," Amy shot back.

"I think you're forgetting how this deal was set up," Adam retorted. "This wasn't a romance. She was providing submission and sex for cash. As long as she gets her money, she's happy."

"Is that really what you think, Adam? Did you see nothing else when she looked at you? Are you really that clueless?"

James put his hand on Amy's arm. "Calm down, sweetheart," he said, his tone gentle but firm. "You're out of line."

"I'm sorry if I am, but you know I'm right. If nothing else, Carly shouldn't have been sent away before I had a chance to examine her. She suffered a significant trauma and was sedated. Adam got her up and out before she could possibly have had a chance to process what she'd been through or figure out what she wanted or needed."

Amy turned again to Adam, her eyes like daggers. "Where did she go, Adam? Where did you send her?"

Adam shrugged, feeling miserable. "I don't know. Jordan's not back yet. I told him to take her wherever she wanted to go."

"Let's all sit down and have some coffee," James suggested. "We'll talk this through."

Adam, glad for something to do, led them back to the kitchen and busied himself making a fresh pot of coffee. While Amy got the cream and sugar, James set the pastries out on the table. When they were all seated in front of their coffee mugs, James turned to Adam. "So what happens now?"

"I don't know," Adam said, feeling as if someone had put lead weights on his chest. "Carly gets her money, I move on. End of story."

Amy frowned, reaching for her cup. Adam tried to ignore her silent reproach.

"What are the terms of the contract?" James, ever the attorney, asked. "Does Carly still get paid if it's terminated early?"

"I think so." Adam shrugged, frowning. "I'll make sure she does."

"May I see the contract?" James asked.

"Sure. Let me get it." Adam went to the study and retrieved the contract, handing it to James.

He sat again and Amy put her hand on his arm, her touch gentle. "I'm sorry, Adam. I shouldn't have snapped at you. It's just, I saw something between the two of you last night, something that is rare, something that should be nurtured, not nipped in the bud before it has a chance to flower."

"You're romanticizing it, Amy," Adam said sadly. "Carly was a pro, in it for the money. What we had was a business transaction, one that wasn't working out. It's that simple. I learned a long time ago in business when to cut my losses. That's all I was doing."

"Liar," Amy said.

"Excuse me?"

"You heard me. We've known you for over ten years, Adam. We've watched you bring a series of lovely young women home, and time after time, you always find a reason to end it before it gets started. You're so focused on your assumptions that they only want you for your money that you never even give them a chance. James and I never said anything, but this time it's different. Carly was different from those girls and you know it."

Adam started to protest, but Amy cut him off. "Yes, I agree this arrangement was less than satisfactory in terms of romantic potential, but there was something *there*, Adam Wise, and don't you try to deny it or to hide behind claims of some kind of business transaction. So she got into the arrangement for the money, so what? It's time to peel away the scar tissue that covers your heart. Carly meant more to you than just a hired piece of ass. Look me in the eye and tell me different."

Amy's words were like arrows pricking Adam's defenses. He felt a lump rising in his throat and realized with embarrassed horror that he was about to cry.

"I shouldn't have sent her away," Adam said in a hoarse voice, surprised how relieved he was to admit this. "I didn't know what else to do."

James put the contract on the table. "You know," he said gently, "sometimes people fuck up, Adam. Lord knows, Amy and I have had our share of issues over the years. You've often said you admire how strong our relationship is. It's because we don't give up. Love isn't a business transaction. It's not something you just walk away from, cutting your losses, as you call it, and moving on. Not when there's something there worth saving. Both Amy and I saw the way you and Carly were looking at each other last night, before things got out of hand. Whatever was going on between the two of you, money was the least of it."

He picked up the contract again, scanning it. "That said, according to this contract, the slave will be paid upon satisfactory completion of the term. I interpret that to mean Carly won't get her money from the auction house until the end of the month. What happens over the next three weeks? She'd expected to spend that time with you. Does she have other arrangements now that you've sent her away?"

"I honestly have no idea. I didn't think about that. Surely she has *somewhere* to go." But did she? A fragment of an earlier conversation returned to him. *Don't send me back. Please. I have nowhere to go.* He'd assumed at the time she was being overly dramatic, but what if it was true?

"So what do I do now? Now that it's too late?" Adam asked miserably.

"It's never too late, Adam," Amy said. "Not when love is at stake."

Chapter 13

Twenty-two dollars and fourteen cents. Carly felt in the bottom of her purse for any loose change and added another quarter and a nickel to the count.

Oh wait, there was the money she kept hidden away for emergencies. Carly opened the glove compartment and rooted beneath the maps and the car owner's manual for her stash. Shit, was that all there was? Seven dollars in single bills and quarters. How could she possibly survive on twenty-nine dollars and change for the next three weeks?

She glanced at the car clock — not quite eight o'clock. The front offices wouldn't open until nine. Did she dare let them know she'd been terminated? Adam had assured her he would make sure she got paid, but did he really have any control over that?

She'd been so muddled and shocked after his pronouncement that he wanted her gone that she hadn't had the presence of mind to demand that he accompany her to the auction house to make sure she got her money, or at the very least have him place a phone call to someone in authority. She'd thought of it only as Jordan was driving away in the sleek, black sedan after having deposited her beside the 1983 junk heap that held all her worldly possessions.

Reaching into her purse, Carly fished for her cell phone. But she didn't know Adam's number. Not only that, the battery was dead. Even if she did get it charged, with her luck they had probably cut off her service, since she was two months behind in paying the bill.

How had it come to this? Was she really to be reduced to some kind of homeless bag lady sleeping in her car, rummaging through dumpsters behind restaurants in search of stale donuts and open bottles of flat soda?

Stop it. Think. You can get through this. It's just a setback.

She would wait until the auction house office opened, then she'd just explain the situation and ask if she could be paid early. Reaching for her copy of the contract, which Master Franklin had slipped into the outer pocket of her suitcase the night of the auction, she scanned the document, looking for the payout terms.

She realized she was biting her lower lip and quickly stopped herself. Then she snorted and said aloud, "Fuck you, Adam Wise. I'll bite my damn lip all I want."

Just saying his name, though, made tears well in her eyes. Angrily, she wiped them away and forced herself to focus on the contract, just in case she'd missed something she could use to her advantage, but she couldn't seem to concentrate. Her mind felt as if it were filled with fog.

Coffee, she told herself. *I'll buy a cup of coffee while I wait for the office to open.*

Stepping out from the car, she locked the doors and tucked the keys into her purse. It was the first day of autumn, she realized, glancing up at the sunny, blue sky. As if the weather had checked the calendar, today was the first really cool morning of the season, and Carly, wearing only a blouse and jeans, hugged herself, shivering slightly as she crossed the parking lot in the direction of the donut shop located across the street from the auction house.

As she waited in line for her coffee, Carly tried to keep her mind on the future, but the recent past insisted on front and center stage in her brain. She could almost feel Adam's hands on her breasts. He had beautiful hands, with long, tapered fingers that worked incredible magic on her nipples, teasing and tweaking them until she had felt like she could orgasm just from his touch.

She thought about the spanking that first night—how he'd cupped his palm in such a way to increase the sting, how each smack had reverberated in her cunt, leaving her trembling and moaning, not just from erotic pain, but from a dark desire that burned like smoldering embers deep inside her.

And afterwards—the way he'd held her in his arms, letting her hide her face against his strong, smooth chest. She had felt so safe there, so peaceful, despite her stinging ass and thighs, despite the fact she knew she meant nothing to him. If there was a particular moment when she'd crossed the line in her head, letting her guard down so he could slip inside her dreams, it was that first night when he'd held her so sweetly.

Beyond the sweetness, there was his power and his passion. She'd understood for the first time on a gut level what it meant to submit to a strong, dominant man. He'd pulled reactions and feelings from her she hadn't realized she was capable of. He'd made her soar on wings of erotic suffering and submission that transcended pain and went beyond pleasure, filling her with an unfamiliar, fierce joy that was as pure and blinding as liquid sunlight.

How was that possible?

How could he have regarded her as just another girl toy, and yet have bound her to him so thoroughly and so completely in just a few days? How was she going to move past him—to forget him, to find the strength to keep going in the face of such a loss?

"What can I get you?"

Carly found herself standing in front of the counter. It took her a second to even remember why she was in line. "Coffee," she said. "Small, light and sweet."

"Donuts? Bagels? A breakfast sandwich?" queried the bored teenager behind the counter. Carly's stomach rumbled at the mention of food, but she shook her head. She'd get something later at a supermarket—something more affordable.

"No thanks, just the coffee." Carly counted out the coins and placed them on the counter. Once she had her coffee she sat on a stool by the window, staring blankly at the passersby as she sipped the hot, sweet drink, waiting for the auction house doors to open.

When she was done, she went into the public restroom and used the toilet. While washing her hands, she examined herself in the mirror. There were circles under her eyes and her hair was a mess, as usual. She splashed water on her face and rummaged in her purse, using the lipstick she found as rouge, rubbing in the color on her cheekbones and then adding some to her lips. She pulled her fingers through her curls, but quickly gave that up.

She touched the red leather collar still around her neck. The collar! How could she have forgotten her collar? How had Adam forgotten it when he'd sent her away? She reached back beneath her hair, fingering the padlock Adam had placed there that first night.

She realized with a pang that she didn't want to take it off. At the same time she knew that she would.

The collar was a symbol of his ownership, of her submission, of the kind of belonging she'd fooled herself into believing she might actually share with Adam Wise.

He probably had twenty more just like it in some drawer in his big fucking house, ready to place around the next poor idiot's neck, once he got over his supposed misgivings regarding using another human being like a blow-up fuck toy.

Carly welcomed the anger that was blooming inside her, praying it would push away at least a little bit of her heartbreak and despair.

~*~

Adam walked James and Amy out to their car. "Let us know what's going on, won't you, Adam?" Amy said, as he opened her door for her.

"Yeah, I will."

As soon as I figure it out myself, he thought, as he watched them drive away. He had sent Carly away to protect her. What he'd done was wrong—violating the trust of a person who had literally entrusted him with her life. He'd told himself he was doing the right thing, the noble thing.

He'd told himself a lie.

At the core of this whole thing was his cowardice. He was afraid—no, make that terrified—to love again. Though the setup was a little different—with him actually buying a woman outright with cold hard cash, rather than taking her out for expensive dinners and sending her flowers as part of a seduction he never planned to take past its initial stages—the net result was still the same. He'd used his position and his power to keep anyone from getting too close, and it was a pattern he'd been executing for the last twenty years.

He'd been playing what he'd thought of as an exciting, edgy game, but that game had gotten out of control. It had hurt the first woman to cut her way through what Amy had so aptly called the scar tissue around his heart.

Now he felt raw and exposed—vulnerable in a way he hadn't experienced in a very long time. And while it scared the shit out of him, something else seemed to be at play, something unfamiliar but not entirely unwelcome.

It took him a while to tease out what the feeling was, this jittery, almost giddy feeling of possibility. He wasn't completely sure, but he thought it might be…hope.

Adam walked back to the garages and climbed the stairs to the apartment above them where Jordan lived. He knocked on the door and a moment later Jordan pulled it open.

"Hey, boss. What's up? Did I forget an engagement?"

Adam usually gave Jordan an itinerary for the day via an email the night before. He shook his head. "No. I just wanted to ask you a few questions about this morning."

"Want to come in? I just made coffee." Jordan stepped back, gesturing with a hand for Adam to enter.

"No, that's okay." Now that he'd made his decision, Adam felt a sense of urgency. "I just need to know where you took Carly this morning. Where did you drop her off?"

"Back to the auction house."

"The auction house? You didn't take her to her home?"

Jordan shook his head. "She had me drop her off at her car, which was parked in the back of the lot behind the place."

"Her car," Adam repeated. Carly could have gone anywhere from there. Adam had no idea where she lived or worked. He didn't know if she had siblings, if she'd ever been married, what her favorite food was, or any of the little details that make up a life. How had he spent nearly a week with this woman, almost 24/7, and know next to nothing about her?

"Yeah," Jordan said. "A real clunker."

"Excuse me?"

"Her car. At least twenty years old. One of Ford's crappier models, most of the paint chipped and what's left faded to a dull gray. There was a clothing rack across the back seat with a bunch of stuff hanging on it. And the rest of the car was crammed full of stuff. Like someone who's moving across country, or who..." He hesitated.

"Go on," Adam urged. "What?"

"Like someone who doesn't have a home. Someone who lives in their car."

Adam was quiet, absorbing this. Again her words floated back to him—*I have nowhere to go.*

How was that possible? Carly had been obviously intelligent and educated. She was beautiful and well-spoken. How could someone like that live in their *car?*

Jordan must have seen the skepticism and confusion on Adam's face, because he offered, "These days that's not so unheard of, you know." As Adam nodded, Jordan continued, "It's a tough world out there, boss. Lots of people who had good paying jobs for years have found themselves out of work and out of luck. For most people, your last paycheck is it—lose that, and you lose the ability to pay your rent, make your car payment, even buy food for your kids."

Adam thought about this. While he knew intellectually how lucky he was to have never known a day of want, it had never really struck a visceral chord with him until now. He tried to imagine Carly living and sleeping in her car, and failed. Wherever she was now, it was Adam's fault. He'd sent away the best thing to ever fall into his life.

His father used to say, "Whoever said money can't buy you happiness just didn't have *enough* money. Money can buy you whatever you want, boy, and don't you forget it." Adam hadn't forgotten it, but for the first time in his life, he found himself questioning his father's wisdom. Money had "bought" him Carly, but now she was gone, and it might be too late to get her back.

It's never too late, Adam. Not when love is at stake.

"I'm taking the Porsche," Adam said. "I won't need you the rest of the day."

~*~

Leaving the restroom, Carly saw on the store clock that it was nine o'clock at last. She left the donut shop, heading toward the auction house, determined to make her case.

She didn't need Adam Wise. She didn't even *want* him, not anymore. This past week had been a fantasy—an intense, dark, thrilling, but ultimately empty fantasy. It was time to get back to real life. It was time to move on.

Resolutely, Carly pushed through the glass doors of the auction house building. The reception area looked like any other place of business, with a waiting area of comfortable chairs positioned around a coffee table laden with magazines. The receptionist, a stunning redhead with the elegant voluptuousness of a fifties film star, was seated behind the gleaming silver curve of the high counter, staring intently at her computer monitor.

She looked up as the tinkle of bells on the door signaled Carly's entry. For a moment her face was a polite blank, and then Gina recognized Carly and she smiled quizzically. "Carly! What're you doing here? I thought you were on assignment?"

Carly approached the counter, glad they were alone. "I am—er, I was. There was, um, a problem. A situation." As Gina's smile faded to a frown, Carly said hurriedly, "I need to talk to Mistress Audrey. Is she available?" Carly didn't want to speak to Master Franklin. She could already imagine his disapproving countenance as he listened to her. He would instantly assume the fault lay entirely with her. At least with the more compassionate Audrey, Carly felt she had a chance to plead her case.

Gina shook her head. "The trainers aren't in this week. The next auction isn't until next month." She tilted her head toward Carly, her expression sympathetic. "Gee, what happened? Must have been bad, huh, that you're back so soon?"

Carly nodded glumly. "Yeah," she whispered, afraid she might burst into tears if she said any more.

Taking pity, Gina said, "Do you want to see Mr. Butler? He's in. I could see if he's available." Carly's stomach sank at the mention of Mr. Butler. Jack Butler was the owner of *Erotica Auctions*, and Carly had seen enough of him in action to know he was the last person she wanted to talk to.

Over the course of the training week he appeared from time to time to watch one of the slaves being put through her paces. Without exception, his remarks about their behavior were disparaging and dismissive. Toward the end of the week, he'd had the girls line up in a row, while he walked up and down in front of them, noting each one's imperfections and failures, his words scathing, his tone cutting. When he was done, he turned to the trainers and announced that this was without a doubt the worst crop of slaves the auction house had seen in a decade, and the auction house would be lucky just to make back the money it had invested in trying to train their sorry asses.

Mistress Audrey had later confided to the girls that Mr. Butler said that with every new group of girls—he came from the school of thought that fear and humiliation were the best training tools, something, thankfully, the trainers did not agree with.

Carly started to tell Gina she would check back later, when the door to the back offices opened and Jack Butler appeared. He was a big man, with broad shoulders and a thick neck—the kind of man who had probably been an athlete in his college days, but was now running to fat.

"What seems to be the problem here, Gina," Mr. Butler began, before cutting himself off as he looked critically at Carly. "You are slave Carly. I recognize you even with your clothes on. What are you doing here? Aren't you supposed to be out on assignment?"

Seizing the moment, Carly nodded. "Yes, Sir. I'm supposed to be, but there's, um, there's been a problem. I was hoping to discuss it with Mistress Audrey or—"

"A problem? Damn right there's a problem, since you're standing here in my offices, instead of naked and on your knees in your Master's home."

"I need to explain—"

"You do, indeed. Follow me, slave Carly." Without waiting to see if she obeyed, the man turned and retreated into his office. Carly glanced at Gina, who gave an apologetic shrug. Aware this probably wasn't going to go well, but not sure what else to do, Carly walked around the reception counter and entered the owner's gleaming chrome and leather space.

Mr. Butler sat behind a desk made of a huge slab of polished black marble on shiny metal legs. He pointed toward one of the chairs in front of the desk and waited while Carly sat nervously on the edge of the seat.

"Go on," Mr. Butler said, pursing his lips and tenting his fingers beneath his chin. His pale blue eyes were like chips of flint in his pudgy face. "I'm listening."

Carly took a deep breath and plunged in, trying to ignore the man's icy glare. "I'm here because my, uh, Master, decided that this setup wasn't right for him. He assured me I would be paid in full, but he, uh, he just didn't want to keep me for the full thirty days." She felt tears welling in her eyes and blinked them rapidly away, refusing to cry in front of this bastard. "He doesn't want a refund or anything like that," she hurried on. "I just wanted to make sure I'd, uh, you know, be paid in full. I could really use the money. I was hoping I could be paid now."

Her voice had trailed off to a whisper under his stern gaze and she found herself looking down at her lap, feeling like a child making excuses in the principal's office. A hot tear splashed onto her hands.

"It's not quite that simple, young lady." Apparently unmoved, Mr. Butler swiveled toward his computer monitor and began to tap on his keyboard. As Carly sat waiting, she felt the impotent anger rising in her like bile, burning in her throat and making her eyes water.

"I see this is your first stint with us. Needless to say it will be your last."

Carly bit her tongue to keep from retorting that he could bet his ass it would be her last. He hadn't said no yet. She clung to that thread of hope and kept her mouth shut while he continued to tap away at his computer.

Finally he reached for the telephone on his desk and pushed the intercom button.

"Yes, sir?" Carly heard Gina say from the other room.

"Get me client Adam Wise on the phone. You can put it directly through." He turned to Carly, his tone cold. "I'm sure you appreciate I need to speak with your Master before we go any further. For all I know, you are in disgrace and running from that fact, trying to collect on services you've failed to render."

Indignant, Carly began, "No, that isn't—"

"Silence," the man roared, holding his palm outward in her direction. "While in this auction house, you are a slave, and you will behave accordingly, regardless of whether you failed in your duties elsewhere."

"I didn't—"

The phone on the man's desk rang, and he reached for it, cutting Carly off with his brusque, "Yes?" He listened a moment and then said, "Very well, call back and leave him a message to call me as soon as possible regarding the matter of his contract with *Erotica Auctions*."

Hanging up the phone, he turned back to Carly. "As I said, I will need to speak with your Master to determine the veracity of your claims. If he corroborates your story, you will be paid at the end of the term, a little more than three weeks' time. If he has any complaint *whatsoever* about your training or behavior, the payment terms of the contract as far as you are concerned are rendered null and void. You knew that going in, slave Carly. A good slave pleases her Master in all things. You clearly failed to do so."

Carly opened her mouth to protest, her cheeks scalding, her heart racing. She realized she was sputtering, too flustered and outraged to say anything coherent, anything that this smug, self-satisfied son of a bitch would hear. She felt lightheaded, the blood roaring in her ears as she stood, moving on wooden legs out of his office, ignoring Gina's questioning glance as she pushed her way blindly out of the building.

Chapter 14

Carly walked quickly around to the back of the building toward the lot where her car waited. She had to lean against the back wall of the building for several minutes until her head cleared and her breathing returned to normal. Though her eyes were hot with unshed tears, she refused to give the smug bastard sitting inside the satisfaction of crying.

Instead, she reminded herself how strong she was. She'd been independent since she was eighteen. She'd been exposed to misogynistic assholes many times before, especially some of the entitled attorneys at the law office where she'd worked. She'd been a New Yorker for the last decade. She could take anything anyone decided to dish out, and come out fighting.

Screw Jack Butler, screw Adam Wise.

Even as this thought moved like a whip through her mind, she knew underneath her anger and her pain that she could trust Adam to keep his word. Even if he'd sent her away without giving her a chance, he wouldn't let the auction house screw her over when it came to her payment. She had to believe this.

All she had to do was hang on another three weeks. She would find friends who would let her crash for a day or two on their couches. She might find temporary work. If absolutely necessary she would sleep in her car. At least it wasn't winter. It would be weeks before she even needed to use the heat. She would be fine.

Then she'd get her money, which would give her some breathing room while she figured out what to do next with her life. She'd drive down to Texas or maybe to Florida. She'd find work. Maybe she'd go to college part time and get a degree in business or something. She was only thirty-two and the world was hers for the taking.

Though that world didn't contain the one man who had somehow slipped deep into her heart, the one man she knew it would take years for her to get over, to put behind her, to forget… Again the tears tried to push their way into her eyes, and again she reminded herself she was strong. She needed no one.

Carly began to walk back to her car, holding on to her new resolve like a lifeline. As she walked she saw a small, sexy sports car pull into the back lot from a side street. Though there were plenty of spaces in the lot, for some reason the car pulled into the space directly beside her car.

As Carly came closer she could see a man in the driver's seat, though because the windows were tinted, she couldn't see his features. Then the car door opened and Carly's heart constricted almost painfully, as if the person stepping out of the car had reached in and squeezed.

Her pride told her to look away, to pretend she hadn't seen the man who had hurt her so badly. She was rooted to the spot, drinking in the sight of him as if it had been years, rather than just hours, since he'd sent her away.

"Carly! Oh, Carly, I'm so glad I found you!"

His words and the expression on his face—a heartbreaking mixture of relief, joy and apprehension—melted the last of her defenses. All self-made promises to put him behind her—to move on and forget the man who had occupied her every waking moment and much of her dreams for the past week—were forgotten in that instant.

Adam stepped out of the car. He was still wearing the same shorts and T-shirt he'd had on early that morning, his cheeks stubbled with five o'clock shadow, his dark hair tousled, his gray eyes burning into hers.

"Adam," Carly whispered, no longer trying to fight the tears that sprang to her eyes and slipped down her cheeks.

Stepping toward her, Adam touched her red slave collar, his eyes softening with sorrow. His hand traveled upward and he stroked away her tears with his thumb, the gesture at once tender and sensual.

Carly tried to muster righteous anger. This man had sent her away without giving her a chance, breaking the contract, breaking her heart. Thanks to him she might well be out of the money owed her. Because of him she'd had to endure that bastard Butler's harangue. Yet in spite of all this, she couldn't seem to stop her lips from lifting into an absurdly happy grin. She had to restrain herself, wrapping her arms around her torso to keep from flinging them around Adam and pulling him close.

"What are you doing here?" she demanded.

"I came to find you." Adam glanced from her to her car and Carly felt herself flushing. She stood straighter, daring him with her eyes to make some rude remark about her car and her obvious dire straits. She readied herself with a sharp retort, something involving silver spoons and entitled bastards.

But Adam made no remark, disparaging or otherwise. Instead he stepped closer to her, reaching for her hand. Though Carly hadn't meant to, she let him take it. The yearning in his face was so palpable that she felt her anger melting away as she lost herself in his gaze. When he pulled her close, she let him, pressing her face against his chest and breathing in his scent, feeling she could stay cocooned in his strong arms for the rest of her life.

When Adam finally let her go, he stepped back, looking around the parking lot as if just realizing where he was. "I saw you walking from the building. Did you get everything squared away with the auction house?"

Carly found herself blurting out the whole story, the words tumbling over themselves as she gave vent to her frustration and outrage. As she spoke, Adam's face grew dark, his mouth drawing down in a frown.

"Let's go," he said, taking her hand. "We'll just straighten this out right now. I don't give a shit what the terms of the contract are, that man had *no* right to talk to you like that. Who the fuck does he think he is?"

They entered the building, Adam bursting through the doors, Carly right behind him. "I need to see Jack Butler," he said to Gina. "Now."

Gina looked from Adam to Carly and back to Adam. She stood abruptly and turned back to Mr. Butler's office, knocking lightly on the door and then slipping inside, closing the door behind her.

A moment later Jack Butler emerged, a small, tight smile on his face. "Mr. Wise. A pleasure," he said, extending his hand.

"We need to talk," Adam replied, not taking the offered hand. "In your office."

"Absolutely," Mr. Butler replied, his tone unctuous. "I apologize for this slave's behavior. We will do everything we can to make things right for you." Turning to Carly, the man added in a sour tone, "You will wait out here, slave Carly."

"No, she will *not* wait out here," Adam retorted, putting his arm around Carly. "This directly concerns her."

Mr. Butler frowned, but bowed slightly in acquiescence as he waved the two of them into his office. He sat again behind his huge desk and leaned forward. "What is this all about, Mr. Wise?"

"What it's about is that I realized I made a mistake in taking on a slave for hire and using her like a sex object without regard or knowledge of her as a human being."

Mr. Butler had again pasted an insincere smile on his face, but his voice was tight. "You were clearly informed of the terms of the contract, Mr. Wise. If you're seeking a return of your deposit it's absolutely—"

Adam shook his head impatiently. "I'm not seeking anything back. You're right—I knew what I was getting into, or I thought I did. I paid the money, and Carly did everything she was supposed to do, and more. She was exemplary in her behavior in every respect."

Carly swallowed, aware this wasn't entirely true, as she'd failed to disclose her claustrophobia until it was too late. She was mutely grateful that Adam didn't bring this up.

"You can keep every dime and you're welcome to it," Adam continued. "I also understand the contract doesn't provide payment to the slave until the term is expired, but I am here to make sure you understand that slave Carly has fulfilled her side of the contract to the letter, and she *will* be paid what is owed her when it's due. Are we both crystal clear on that?"

"Clear as a bell," Mr. Butler said through clenched teeth, the smile on his face now decidedly a grimace.

Adam stood, holding out his hand to Carly. "Good. That's all I wanted to hear." It was all Carly could do to hide her smile as they left the office and the building.

They walked together in silence toward their cars, Carly's hand still clasped in Adam's. While she was delighted at the way Adam had handled Mr. Butler, the whole morning had been such a crazy rollercoaster of ups and downs that she was in something of a daze.

When they reached their cars, Adam dropped her hand and turned to her. "Carly," he whispered, tears filling his eyes. "I'm so, so sorry. I really fucked up. I shouldn't have sent you away like that. I know now how close I came to losing you. I'm hoping against hope you'll give me a second chance. Do you think that's even remotely possible?"

Carly's reply was pulled from her like a sigh, as Adam took her into his arms. "Yes," she said. "Yes."

~*~

They were quiet as they drove along the parkway toward Scarsdale. Adam kept glancing at Carly, not quite believing he had her back, stunned at how easily he'd let her go.

"What do I do about my car?" Carly suddenly said.

It took Adam a second to process what she was asking. "I'll send Jordan for it. You can keep it at my place."

Carly nodded. Adam continued to glance every few seconds toward the passenger seat to make sure she was actually there, and not part of some daydream.

"What?" Carly finally said, her face breaking into a tentative smile as she met his gaze.

"You."

"Me?" Carly gave him a quizzical look.

Adam laughed. "I'm sorry. I just can't keep my eyes off you. I can't believe how incredibly stupid I was. I feel like a guy on death row who got a reprieve right before they inserted the lethal injection."

A faint blush moved over Carly's cheeks. "So what happens now?

"Do we pick up where we left off? Finish the contract?" She was staring straight ahead again, her expression difficult to read.

"No. The contract is done."

She glanced his way, her eyes questioning, biting her lower lip.

Adam grinned in spite of himself. So much for training that out of her. Yet now he found the gesture charming—an indication of her vulnerability that made him want to take her into his arms and kiss away all her fears.

"What I mean is," he said, reaching over to touch her knee, "I don't want you back under any kind of contractual terms. I just want you back. I want us to try this thing without the artificial constraints of the auction contract." Recalling her old car stuffed with what appeared to be all her worldly possessions, he hastened to add, "I think we lit enough of a fire under Butler's ass to make sure you get paid everything you're owed when the time comes." He gave a small, mirthless laugh but then sobered. "But regarding *us*, I'm hoping you might see your way to giving this another try on equal footing. As partners."

"Partners?"

"I realize now I used the whole contract thing as a way to keep you at arm's length. I've done that more or less my whole adult life. I don't want to live that way anymore. I want to get to know you. I want you to know me. I want us to take our time—no schedules, no contracts, no deadlines."

They were in his neighborhood now, nearly to his street. At a stop sign, Adam turned to Carly, memorizing every line and plane of her sweet face. "I don't know anything about you, Carly, other than you are submissive and masochistic, beautiful, intelligent, articulate, sensual and the sexiest woman I ever met."

Carly laughed, a deep, throaty laugh filled with happiness, her eyes crinkling into half moons, her cheeks dimpling. Adam realized he'd never heard her laugh before and that he wanted to hear it again, and often. "That's it, huh?" she finally said, still grinning.

Adam found himself laughing too, the sudden lightness inside nearly lifting him from his seat. She hadn't said yes, but she hadn't said no. She was there beside him, smiling at him, and he realized that was enough.

~*~

Carly's stomach clenched as she followed Adam across the threshold and into the imposing marble foyer of his house. Adam closed the door behind them and turned to her, taking her into his arms. He lowered his head, touching his lips to hers. It wasn't their first kiss—there was the dream kiss that one night when she'd dared to sidle up beside him, aching with loneliness, needing to feel a man's arms around her. But it was, she decided, their first conscious kiss, their first kiss as equals.

She let her lips part as Adam's tongue eased sweetly into her mouth. He pulled her closer, crushing her breasts to his chest, his hands cupping her ass as his kiss became more insistent. She could feel his erection, hard against her thigh. A delicious, sweet heat moved through her body, making her heart pound.

When at last he pulled back, Carly found herself leaning forward, her mouth suddenly bereft from the loss of his kiss, her body cold without his surrounding warmth. "Carly, I have to have you. Now." Adam's voice was hoarse. Carly opened her eyes as he moved to her side, reaching to lift her into his arms.

He held her close as he moved into the living room. Setting her down on a large sofa, he knelt beside her, his fingers fumbling at the buttons on her blouse. Within seconds he had it open. His expression was hungry, almost fierce, as he tugged at her bra, pulling it upward so her breasts sprang free, his mouth closing over one nipple, lips, teeth and tongue bringing it to an instant, aching erection. As he suckled, his hands sought her jeans, tugging at the snap, dragging the zipper down, pulling the denim, along with her underwear, down her legs.

Carly was breathless, her heart beating fast. Adam stood just long enough to pull his shirt over his head. Carly reached behind her back, released the clasps of her bra and tossed it to the floor. Sitting up, she reached for Adam's fly, pulling it open. Hooking her fingers on either side, she tugged at his shorts, slipping them past his narrow hips. His erection bobbed toward her, its tip glistening. Leaning forward, Carly closed her lips over the head, savoring the taste and feel of him.

As she sucked the length of his shaft into her mouth, she wrapped her arms around him, pulling him closer. She would never have dared to take such liberties just a few hours earlier, but he had said they were to be partners—equals, and this was exactly and precisely what she wanted—no, what she needed—to do.

He stood in her embrace for several long moments, his fingers twining in her curls as she worshipped his cock. "I need to be inside you, Carly," he finally rasped, releasing her hair and pushing her back against the sofa. Kneeling in front of her, he lifted her onto the cushion.

Carly held out her arms and Adam fell on top of her, his mouth again finding hers, his kiss even more urgent than before. His cock pressed hard against her wetness. She arched up, pulling him into her, aching to be filled, his name pulled from her lips as he entered her. She felt his hand on her throat, the primal, dominant gesture sending spirals of melting, submissive lust through every inch of her body. He moved in a perfect swivel inside her, his pubic bone rubbing against her throbbing clit with each thrust.

"Open your eyes," he commanded in a deep voice. "Look at me." Carly forced her eyes to flutter open, trying to focus, trying to catch her breath. Adam's eyes were bright, lit with that inner fire she'd seen a few times before, but along with the fire was something new, something vulnerable, even pleading.

"Carly," he whispered throatily, his voice breaking. "My darling, my love. Come for me. Now."

She did.

~*~

The snow was falling thickly outside, blanketing the lawn and trees, fat flakes drifting past the windows. Inside the fire crackled in the hearth, its flames rouging the cheeks of the two couples sitting comfortably around the hearth.

It was the last day of the year, and Adam and Carly had invited James and Amy to celebrate. They'd enjoyed a delicious meal prepared in advance by Adam's cook and were having their coffee by the fire.

Adam set down his cup and turned to Carly. "It's time, slave girl." He touched the O-ring on her collar, looping his finger into it and tugging gently. Carly felt herself slip immediately into the all-encompassing submissive state of being that came more and more easily to her as the weeks with Adam had eased into months. Everything extraneous seemed to slide away, her focus solely on her Master.

"Kneel, head down, arms out."

Carly moved from the sofa to the carpet in a fluid movement, kneeling with her forehead to the ground, her arms stretched in front of her. She could hear the murmuring of James, Amy and her Master above her but she didn't pay attention to the words. She had entered a different plane, an altered state of being.

She stayed still, her mind emptying, a deep sense of calm moving over her. She felt the hem of her dress being lifted, and the warmth of the fire on her bare skin. Adam's hand moved over her ass and she let out a breath, reveling in his touch, content to wait for his next command.

They had talked about tonight and what he would expect from her. They had been working toward this moment for the last month, his knowledge of her triggers and limits deepening, her trust and ability to move through her fears stronger with each passing day. They had agreed they wanted witnesses for this new level of submission, and neither could think of anyone better to invite than James and Amy.

She felt Adam's hand on the back of her neck, her signal to rise. Carly lifted herself upright and stood. James, Amy and Adam were all standing as well. The men were both fully dressed in jeans and button down shirts. The women wore silky shifts that came to the knee, their nipples clearly outlined against the sheer fabric, both of them barefoot in the warmth of Adam's comfortable house. Neither showed any sign of self-consciousness. Each understood that her body was a gift for her Master, never to be concealed or withheld.

They walked together to the basement, James and Adam leading the way, Amy and Carly following behind. As they walked, Amy slipped her hand into Carly's and squeezed. Carly glanced at her, smiling, and Amy smiled back, her eyes twinkling.

Adam led them through the basement to the water chamber beyond, where he and Carly had spent many hours working through Carly's fears and exploring her secret desires. Tonight they would go further than they had before. She was ready, she had assured him that morning as they snuggled in bed, her trust in him, and more importantly in herself, absolute.

James and Amy took their seats on folding chairs Adam had brought into the chamber earlier that afternoon. The top was off the water tank, the water inside heated to a comfortable, soothing temperature. Adam touched the thin strap of Carly's shift, pushing it gently from her shoulder. Following his lead, she pushed the other strap, letting the dress puddle at her feet.

Gently Adam tugged at the golden hoops in her nipples, both of which stiffened at his touch. She stood straight and proud, meeting his gaze with a smile, melting at the warmth and love she saw in his eyes.

The nipple piercing had been an early Christmas gift to her. Instead of responding with fear and white-knuckling her way through it, Adam had helped her to embrace the experience, to accept the sudden, sharp pain of the needle's tip as the price of wearing his rings. Her nipples had healed beautifully, and she couldn't help but admire the rosy gold rings every time she showered or glanced down at her breasts while they lay naked together in bed. She knew she would get used to them in time, but she would always regard them as shiny gold talismans that signified the sparkling joy of her new life with Adam Wise.

Adam unbuttoned his shirt and let it fall from his shoulders. He slipped out of his jeans, revealing black silk bikini underwear, his sexy bulge straining beneath the fabric. He retrieved two coils of soft nylon rope from the supply cabinet and went to the water tank, climbing the sturdy stairs that led to the platforms on either side of the tank. Kneeling, he reached down his hand, which Carly took as she mounted the stairs.

Her heart quickened as she climbed, but none of the old paralyzing, blinding fear she'd once experienced at the thought of being confined in a small space resurfaced, even though she knew what they were about to do. She glanced toward James and Amy, aware of the concern in Amy's eyes, smiling when James took Amy's hand in his and pulled her close, as if to say, *Don't worry. It's all okay.*

And it was all okay. Better than okay. The willing exchange of power between Adam and Carly was more powerful than anything she'd experienced with other dominant men in the past, men who knew what it was to take, but had little concept of what it was to give, truly give, of one's heart and soul. Adam had taught her that it was possible to be both equal and submissive; that strength and submission were not opposites, but blended together to create something powerful and enduring. He showed her daily how much he valued the gift of her submission, and she in turn treasured his dominance.

Carly knelt on the wide platform beside the tank, lifting her arms so Adam could slip the padded canvas harness over her head. Heavy iron weights had been sewn inside the pads along the front of the harness to assure she sank beneath the water. The weights tugged Carly forward and she shifted on her knees to maintain her balance as Adam adjusted the harness over her torso.

Carly had worn the harness during other sessions in the water tank, but she'd never been bound at the same time. Tonight would be different. Silently Carly prayed for the grace and courage to do what came next. She brought her arms behind her back while Adam crouched behind her.

He wound the rope around her arms, starting at the top and working his way toward her wrists. As the rope snugged around her, Carly felt a sensuous calm settling over her as she moved into the submissive headspace where nothing existed except Adam and herself, and whatever task he had set before her.

When she was thoroughly bound, he reached for the fat metal clips that dangled from the winch embedded in the ceiling beam. Carefully he attached the clips to the D rings sewn at intervals along the sides of the harness. Finally he placed thick, soft leather cuffs around Carly's ankles and thighs, attaching additional winch clips to the O rings on each cuff.

When Carly was properly secured, Adam nodded towards James, who now stood beside the wall ratchet that controlled the winch. James began to turn the winch wheel, lifting Carly into the air until she hung parallel to the water shimmering a few feet below her.

Pulling off his underwear, Adam eased himself into the water. "I love you, Carly," he said softly, reaching up to cup her face in his hands.

"I love you, Sir."

"Are you ready for the submersion, slave girl?" he asked in a louder voice.

"Yes, Sir." A tremor moved through Carly's frame and she swayed gently in the weighted harness, cuffs and rope. Yes, she was afraid, but at the same time she was determined to go through with this ultimate exercise in submission.

"When I count to three, take a deep breath and hold it. You will stay calm and still beneath the water. You will not struggle. I will decide when you breathe again. Are we clear on this?"

"Yes, Sir," Carly breathed, her heart beating a rapid tattoo against her bones.

Adam reached up, stroking her cheek. He spoke again in a soft voice, meant for her ears alone. "Easy. Slow. Remember our work. Remember your grace."

Carly nodded, closing her eyes, focusing on her love for this man, drawing on the courage she knew was inside her. "Tell me what your safe cue is," Adam said.

Carly's voice, when she spoke, seemed to her to be disembodied, but at least it didn't quiver. "If I feel scared or about to panic, I'm to nod my head up and down, like this." Carly demonstrated, feeling slightly silly, though at the same time aware how important this was.

Adam nodded in approval. "Good. Remember, I will be right beside you in the water. I will be watching and paying attention." He touched her cheek again. "Ready?"

Carly nodded, not quite trusting herself to speak again.

"One," Adam said.

James began to turn the winch, lowering Carly toward the water.

"Two."

She hovered just above the tank. Closing her eyes, she drew in a deep breath, filling her lungs, emptying her mind.

"Three."

Carly descended into the warm silence of the water, the weights pulling her down. Though she sensed Adam near her, she didn't open her eyes. The fear that had assailed her as she swayed above the tank had evaporated, leaving only the rush of adrenaline it had left in its aftermath. She realized she was counting. *One thousand, two thousand, three thousand...*

Her chest felt tight, a burning sensation moving through her lungs.

Twenty-one, twenty-two...

Her heart pounded. All she had to do was nod her head and he'd pull her to safety.

She didn't do it.

A curious, peaceful calm moved over her and she let her body go limp, her muscles and bones sliding from her skin, flowing into the water, becoming one with it.

I love Adam. I trust him with my love, with my heart, with my life...

All at once the air hit Carly and her eyes flew open. She hung suspended for a few seconds, and then was lowered onto the platform, Adam's hands guiding her down. As her mind switched back on, she realized Amy was beside Adam, both of them moving quickly to release the clips, unwind the rope, pull the heavy harness from her body.

A thick, warm towel was wrapped around her and she felt herself being lifted and then cradled in strong arms. "Carly? You okay, darling?"

She smiled up into Adam's face, a sense of utter joy radiating through her like the purest, sweetest sunlight, warming her from the inside out. "Yes," she breathed. "I'm perfect."

~*~

Later that evening Carly sat snuggled in her bathrobe beside Adam, her cheeks rosy, her eyes sparkling. Adam reached for her hand, lifting it to his lips and kissing her palm. James and Amy sat across from them, their shared, secret looks no longer a mystery to Adam Wise. He understood now what it meant to have a heart so full it felt like it might burst. He realized that, despite what he'd thought all these years, he'd never really been in love. Not the kind of love that you would die for, but would rather live for — the kind of love story that never has an ending.

James had added several logs to the fire. The flames leaped and curled against the wood. Amy set the crystal champagne flutes on the glass table between the two sofas while Adam lifted the bottle from the ice bucket and twisted at the wire holding the cork in place.

The grandfather clock in the corner of the living room began to chime and they all turned to listen. At the twelfth stroke, Adam popped the cork, filled their glasses and handed them around.

He lifted his glass and the others lifted theirs as well. "To friends," he said first, smiling and nodding toward James and Amy. In the months since Carly had returned to him, Adam had found the shields he hadn't realized he'd erected around himself falling away, no longer needed. He'd been able to hear and accept James' gentle coaching and advice as he learned how to be a real Dom for Carly, instead of just for himself.

"To a new year," he continued, caressing Carly with his gaze. "To new life, new beginnings and most of all, to love."

Also Available at Romance Unbound Publishing (http://romanceunbound.com)

The Story of Owen: One Man's Submissive Journey
Sold into Slavery
Caught: Punished by Her Boss
Slave Academy
Tough Boy
Enslaved
Princess
Heart Thief
Slave Island
Alternative Treatment
Switch
Dream Master
The Cowboy Poet
Safe in His Arms
Heart of Submission
The Solitary Knights of Pelham Bay – The Series
Texas Surrender
Unleashed Magic
Sarah's Awakening
Wicked Hearts

Submission Times Two
Confessions of a Submissive
A Princely Gift
Accidental Slave
Slave Girl
Lara's Submission
Slave Jade
Obsession: Girl Abducted
Golden Angel: Unwilling Sex Slave
The Toy
Frog: A Tale of Sexual Torture

Connect with Claire

Website: http://clairethompson.net
Romance Unbound Publishing:
http://romanceunbound.com
Twitter: http://twitter.com/CThompsonAuthor
Facebook:
http://www.facebook.com/ClaireThompsonauthor

Made in the USA
Middletown, DE
04 November 201